"WHAT ARE YOU DOING?" SHE DEMANDED.

"This," whispered Cam, placing his lips into the curve of her long neck.

Her pulse careened wildly beneath his lips. Julia trembled. She tried to tamp her rising excitement, but the exquisite pleasure of his touch defeated her. She felt her resistance melting away with each long smooth stroke of his hands over her arms.

This man knows what he's doing! flashed through Julia's mind, but even that cynical thought didn't stop her from responding to his well-placed kisses and his calculated caresses.

Julia heard a low sigh, nearly a moan, and was surprised to recognize that it came from her own lips. She was overwhelmed by the urgent need to touch him, to thread her fingers through his hair, to surrender to this dangerously desirable man.

A CANDLELIGHT ECSTASY ROMANCE ®

90 BREATHLESS SURRENDER, *Kay Hooper*
91 SPELLBOUND, *Jayne Castle*
92 CRIMSON MORNING, *Jackie Black*
93 A STRANGE ELATION, *Prudence Martin*
94 A WAITING GAME, *Diana Blayne*
95 JINX LADY, *Hayton Monteith*
96 FORBIDDEN FIRES, *Nell Kincaid*
97 DANCE THE SKIES, *Jo Calloway*
98 AS NIGHT FOLLOWS DAY, *Suzanne Simmons*
99 GAMBLER'S LOVE, *Amii Lorin*
100 NO EASY WAY OUT, *Elaine Raco Chase*
101 AMBER ENCHANTMENT, *Bonnie Drake*
102 SWEET PERSUASION, *Ginger Chambers*
103 UNWILLING ENCHANTRESS, *Lydia Gregory*
104 SPEAK SOFTLY TO MY SOUL, *Dorothy Ann Bernard*
105 A TOUCH OF HEAVEN, *Tess Holloway*
106 INTIMATE STRANGERS, *Denise Mathews*
107 BRAND OF PASSION, *Shirley Hart*
108 WILD ROSES, *Sheila Paulos*
109 WHERE THE RIVER BENDS, *Jo Calloway*
110 PASSION'S PRICE, *Donna Kimel Vitek*
111 STOLEN PROMISES, *Barbara Andrews*
112 SING TO ME OF LOVE, *JoAnna Brandon*
113 A LOVING ARRANGEMENT, *Diana Blayne*
114 LOVER FROM THE SEA, *Bonnie Drake*
115 IN THE ARMS OF LOVE, *Alexis Hill*
116 CAUGHT IN THE RAIN, *Shirley Hart*
117 WHEN NEXT WE LOVE, *Heather Graham*
118 TO HAVE AND TO HOLD, *Lori Herter*
119 HEART'S SHADOW, *Prudence Martin*
120 THAT CERTAIN SUMMER, *Emma Bennett*
121 DAWN'S PROMISE, *Jo Calloway*
122 A SILENT WONDER, *Samantha Hughes*
123 WILD RHAPSODY, *Shirley Hart*
124 AN AFFAIR TO REMEMBER, *Barbara Cameron*
125 TENDER TAMING, *Heather Graham*
126 LEGACY OF LOVE, *Tate McKenna*
127 THIS BITTERSWEET LOVE, *Barbara Andrews*
128 A GENTLE WHISPER, *Eleanor Woods*
129 LOVE ON ANY TERMS, *Nell Kincaid*

LOVE SONG

Prudence Martin

A CANDLELIGHT ECSTASY ROMANCE ®

Published by
Dell Publishing Co., Inc.
1 Dag Hammarskjold Plaza
New York, New York 10017

ISBN: 0-440-14849-9

Printed in the United States of America
First printing—April 1983

To Our Readers:

We have been delighted with your enthusiastic response to Candlelight Ecstasy Romances®, and we thank you for the interest you have shown in this exciting series.

In the upcoming months we will continue to present the distinctive sensuous love stories you have come to expect only from Ecstasy. We look forward to bringing you many more books from your favorite authors and also the very finest work from new authors of contemporary romantic fiction.

As always, we are striving to present the unique, absorbing love stories that you enjoy most—books that are more than ordinary romance.

Your suggestions and comments are always welcome. Please write to us at the address below.

Sincerely,

The Editors
Candlelight Romances
1 Dag Hammarskjold Plaza
New York, New York 10017

CHAPTER ONE

Her hair seemed to flash sunbeams. Cam paused in the threshold and watched the morning light captured in the silken wings tucked neatly in her nape. Too neatly, he thought. Hair that lovely should be free, windblown, ruffled from the caresses of a man's hands. He leaned against the doorframe, settled his hands in the pockets of his chocolate-brown cord slacks, and let his eyes travel slowly downward with all the leisure of a man who enjoys appraising women.

Her profile was classically straight, neat, but not exceptional. Small, straight nose and set chin. Long, lovely neck. His eyes came to the mold of the beige sweater, and Cam straightened with a sense of disappointment. Even with the bulk of the cable-knit, her figure was definitely boyishly slim. Not to his taste. Cam liked his women to have full, rounded bodies. He liked to bury his face in a woman's breasts. He shrugged off his disappointment and strolled forward just in time to hear the realtor's apologies.

"I am sorry for the error, Miss Hollis," she was saying in the extremely nasal midwestern twang that Cam still hadn't got used to, even after three years in Chicago.

"It wasn't your fault, Mrs. O'Neal," said the golden-haired woman as she rose with fluid ease. "Do call me when the next apartment becomes available." She stretched out a long thin arm, shook the realtor's hand, turned, and stepped straight into Cam's waiting chest.

"Oh!" she exclaimed. "Excuse me!"

Cam stood motionless, his ready smile forgotten as he recovered from the shock of looking directly into the face that had formed the unexceptional profile. Large, startled, celestial eyes focused wide upon him; and while one part of him assessed cynically the clever use of dark mascara to enhance their size, deepen their blue, another part just sank into the heavenly depths with sheer masculine appreciation.

It was over in an instant. Those thick darkened lashes flickered over the large eyes, and she stepped back. He presented her with a lopsided smile.

"That's quite all right, Miss . . . Hollis, was it? My fault. I had the advantage of seeing you approach." He placed his hand at her elbow and kept it there as he turned to the realtor. "Is there some problem, Mrs. O'Neal? Something I could help with?"

"No, Mr. Stone. No problem at all," the realtor answered with a bright display of teeth. She stood and moved away from her desk. "We can leave immediately for the showing."

He looked at the young woman beside him. Much to his regret, a cool composure was replacing the surprise on her face. Inching her elbow away from his hand, Miss Hollis answered the question in his eyes. "There really is no problem. We were mistakenly called to view the same apartment, but you are the lucky one. Your name tops mine on the waiting list."

There was a hint of reserve to her words, though they'd been softened by a slight lift of her lips. She had turned and taken two steps before Cam went into action. Only God knew why, but he didn't want to see the end of her yet.

"Miss Hollis," he said in tones that halted her.

She looked at him over her shoulder, a question in the cool blue eyes.

"Come see the apartment with me." He mellowed the command in his voice with a cajoling smile. "Who knows? I might decide not to take it. Then you wouldn't have to make another trip out to see it, and Mrs. O'Neal wouldn't have to go through the spiel twice. Even if I do take the place, what have you got to lose?"

She hesitated, considering the matter. Her head tilted to the side; the fluorescent light twined with the sunlight streaking her hair. Her lips pressed tightly together. Like her eyes, they were too wide, too large for her long narrow face. Just as Cam realized how plain she was her lips parted in a smile that transformed each of her features, creating an overall effect that dazzled him.

"I would like that very much," she said, her voice less remote. "I've wanted to see the inside of one of those brick row houses ever since I first came to Chicago. That is, if Mrs. O'Neal doesn't mind."

After seeing that dazzling smile, Cam felt quite prepared to break arms to get the real estate broker's agreement. Fortunately he didn't need to go to such extremes. Mrs. O'Neal beamed with evident relief to have matters resolved so simply.

"Of course, I don't mind. As Mr. Stone pointed out, it could save us having to make a tour later," she said. Her tone clearly indicated she thought this highly unlikely. She adjusted the name badge on the pocket of her fire-red blazer as she bobbed her graying head at her two clients. "Miss Hollis, this is Mr. Cameron Stone. Mr. Stone, Miss Julia Hollis."

She pivoted and moved away with brisk competence. As they followed, Cam ran his eyes swiftly over the length of Miss Julia Hollis. There wasn't that much to run over, given her petite stature. He noted with displeasure the exceedingly slim hips within the dowdy wool skirt. At least, he consoled himself, she didn't have that god-awful midwestern nasality.

By the glass doors of their realtor's office, the trio halted to collect their coats from a metal rack. Cam was not quite quick enough to help Julia into her camel's hair coat. He watched her knot the belt over her tiny waist with the same deftness she'd slipped into it. Her movements were liquid, each flowing into the other without a discernible pause; even her steps had an effortless grace to them.

He walked beside her, wondering if that were how she would move in bed. He studied the delicately rounded calves of her slender legs and pictured them tangling with his in the same fluent rippling motion. He held open the door of the realtor's car with what he hoped was his most innocuous smile. He had the feeling that one hint of what he was thinking would send golden Julia running. She looked far too proper to indulge in sexual fantasy.

Cam slumped in his bucket seat and impatiently tapped his fingers on his knees. He stared out the window, occasionally catching glimpses of sun-striped Lake Michigan, but he wasn't actually paying much attention to the view. He heard Mrs. O'Neal rattling away, and he was able to pick out a word here and there from the jumble. *Exclusive. Fortunate. Some have waited far longer to move into these apartments.* He watched his drumming fingers and wondered if he wanted to move at all. Until he'd got the realtor's call, he'd totally forgotten about having his name on that list.

They drew up before a row of brick Georgian houses. Cam got out and turned with outstretched hand to help Julia out. She eschewed his hand and eased to her feet. He felt a slight prick of annoyance, but shrugged it away as they followed Mrs. O'Neal up the stone walk.

"Have you been waiting long for a chance to take one of these apartments?" he asked Julia.

"About two years," she replied. "And you?"

Her voice was soft, soothing, hushed. In fact, he thought everything about her had a hushed quality. He wondered if she were Catholic. She would have made a great nun.

"Closer to three," he answered as they entered a white-walled foyer with a gleaming wood floor and wooden steps curving out of sight. Four brass-plated mailboxes were cut into the wall on the right. On the left was a heavy dark wood door. Mrs. O'Neal inserted a key into each of the two locks on this door, then held it open for them to pass through.

Directly before them, across an expanse of plush gray carpet, stood a beautifully carved fireplace; the walnut mantel contrasted with the ivory-white of the walls. He bent his head to tell her he liked it already, and then all his theories about Miss Julia Hollis shattered.

Her eyes held that same startled look they'd had when she'd bumped into him, her lashes fluttering over the clear blue irises. Her mouth, too, curved up and out with animated pleasure, reminding Cam of his five-year-old niece on her birthday. Julia's gaze flew about the room, landing finally at his—and her excitement abruptly died.

"Oh," she said flatly. "You like it too."

He laughed and tugged her into the center of the room. "Don't look so crestfallen. I may hate the rest of it. I happen to be very picky about bathrooms."

She smiled, not really reassured, and he could see that she plainly thought anyone who did not sign the lease instantly was a fool.

Like most houses built at the turn of the century, the rooms were largely proportioned, with high ceilings and carved moldings that made looking up worthwhile. To the left there was a niche that jutted out beyond the rest of the living room, with windows on two of the walls. As Mrs. O'Neal pointed it out Cam heard Julia breathe something. He bent forward.

"Pardon?"

"Oh, nothing," she said, looking embarrassed.

"No, really, you said something about sofas?" He turned on his coaxing smile. "If you're an interior designer or something, I'd appreciate the advice. I'd appreciate it anyway. *If* I took this apartment, I'd like it to look right."

"I'm not a designer," she said quickly. She pulled in her lower lip, staring at the niche as if seeing secret visions there. "But I'd put bright cushiony sofas all around those walls and hang plants from the windows. It'd be marvelous for conversations or reading or meditating."

"Do you meditate?" he asked, then wished he hadn't. It broke the spell, and the aloofness returned to her face.

"Doesn't everyone occasionally?" She turned sharply and followed Mrs. O'Neal down the narrow hall that shot off to the right of the living room.

The hall extended the length of the apartment, from the living room to the kitchen at the very end. Off to the left were doors that led in succession to a bedroom, a bathroom, and another bedroom. Julia inspected every closet, rattled every window latch, tested the bathroom taps, and flushed the toilet. She pointed out deficiencies, commented upon merits.

Cameron contented himself with watching Julia. He was both amazed and amused by the myriad of expressions flying over her thin face.

In the second bedroom he was obediently checking the view Mrs. O'Neal was pointing out when he heard the click of the door and the clap of hands. Cam turned to see Julia gleefully examining herself in a full-length built-in beveled mirror. Coming to stand behind her, he saw the reflection of his amusement just to the side and above the reflection of her excitement. The dark cocoa of his hair matched that of his cord jacket and deepened the liquid brown of his eyes. His open-collar white shirt heightened his tan. She looked startling pale by contrast.

Her eyes met his in the mirror, but then Julia reached out and destroyed the image by pulling the door open.

The passage opened out into a dining room with a wall of windows that again had Julia clapping her hands together. Beyond the dining room the left side of the hall was one gigantic china cabinet, with glass doors closing over shelves on the top and rows of drawers on the bottom. After this came another bedroom, another bathroom, and finally the kitchen.

Peering into everything, Julia told Cam exactly what to put where, what to change, what to keep. He nodded his head and agreed to everything, all the while wondering how she could look so vibrantly kissable one minute and so utterly untouchable the next. She checked the lock on the back door, crossed to rattle the windows, then turned on the tap in the sink. Finally she faced Cam, her hand lightly braced on the countertop.

"Are you married, Mr. Stone?" she inquired casually.

His brows went up. A tinge of pink rose over her cheeks. "No," he answered, amused at her obviousness.

"This is much too large for a single man," she commented.

"Equally so for a single woman," he countered.

She pulled in her lip again. Then she twisted around and looked out through the window above the sink. "You *are* taking it, aren't you?"

He hesitated, surprised at the temptation he felt to say no. He wanted very much to see her face light up again. Suddenly Cam caught himself up short. Dammit, what the hell was going on with him? She had a figure about as sexy as a fifteen-year-old *boy,* for God's sake!

"Yes," he replied.

She slowly came around again. A fixed smile emphasized the width of her overlarge mouth. "Of course. So would I, given the chance." She gave herself a little shake that reminded Cam of a puppy shaking off grass. "I thank you very much for giving me the opportunity to see it, Mrs. O'Neal. Please do call me when the next apartment opens up."

Her tone definitely said good-bye. She started down the passageway, while Mrs. O'Neal began talking to him about papers to sign and other mumbo jumbo. Without apology Cam whirled and sprinted after Julia.

"Wait!" he said. "I'll take you to lunch."

She half turned, a silhouette in the shadows as she looked over her shoulder. Cameron suddenly felt like a fool. Her stance held a question, and he knew she was wondering just what he was up to. The hell of it was, he didn't know himself. He simply stood there, staring back at her.

After what seemed an eternity the feathered wings of her hair fanned outward as she shook her head. "Thank you, Mr. Stone, but no. I should be getting back to work."

"Surely you intend to get some lunch somewhere," he insisted. He wasn't used to feminine rejection, and a stubborn determination was growing within him. He was going to take her to lunch, dammit. He'd never seen a woman who needed it more. She didn't look like she'd had a meal in the last decade. She was, however, walking on. Realizing this, he again bounded after her, pulling her to a halt. Her pale brows rose as she looked down her classic nose at the hand encircling her sleeve. He dropped it reluctantly but began speaking as he did so.

"I was sincere about needing your help in decorating this place. I'm not much good at that sort of thing, and I'd really appreciate it if you could give me a few pointers over lunch."

He thought she was still going to refuse and, short of throwing his body against the door, he didn't see how he could keep her from walking out. Well, the hell with her, he thought, his brows clamping down.

A speculative surprise crossed her face, then she said softly, "Very well. I'd be glad to help."

An unwarranted amount of satisfaction swept through him. His shoulders quirked jauntily. "Great. Well, Mrs. O'Neal, would you mind if I came in later to sign all the necessary forms?"

"Not at all. May I drop you two somewhere?" the realtor asked kindly as she checked the locks.

He named a restaurant in the heart of the Loop, not far from the realtor's offices. Fighting the urge to sit in the back beside the enigmatic Miss Hollis, he began a light discussion on the merits of the apartment he'd just agreed to lease. Only a occasional word came from the backseat and that always in Julia's hushed still voice—not the animated vibrating tones she'd used in the apartment.

Once they were seated opposite a Butcher Block table at the restaurant, he stared at the poised plain woman across from him and tried to figure out just why he had wanted to lunch with her. They both ordered a broccoli quiche, which Cam had recommended. He fiddled restlessly with his flatware, then signaled the waitress and ordered a bottle of wine.

He resumed clicking his spoon and knife together. What the hell had he been thinking, he asked himself. She wasn't his type, not his type at all. A surge of animosity toward Miss Tranquillity swelled up in him. The sooner this damn lunch was over, the better.

"So. Are you a native of Chicago, Mr. Stone?" she inquired in that quiet voice he decided he hated.

"Do I sound like one?" he returned on an ill-tempered snap.

She raised her fair brows. "The city has such a varied population, one never knows," she said mildly.

It sounded like a reproof. One shoulder of his cord jacket lifted on a defiant shrug. "I've been here a few years. I originally transferred here to work for Galaxy," he said. As she eyed him blankly, he expanded tersely. "Galaxy Records. Division of LPA."

"Oh," she said, as if to say "Oh, no."

His knife and spoon abruptly ceased to move. "I suppose," he said scathingly, "you're one of those poor souls who thinks Barry Manilow is rock 'n' roll."

"No," she denied, studying him seriously. "I'm one of those poor souls who thinks Frank Sinatra is rock 'n' roll. I haven't much musical taste—or interest—I'm afraid."

Her apologetic air, coupled with the disarming smile, mollified him. He offered his own apology with his particular brand of practiced charm, then went on. "When Galaxy shut down their local offices eighteen months ago, I decided to stay on in Chicago and go into business for myself. I've developed quite a liking for the Windy City. In fact," he added with his most engaging smile, "I'm finding I like it more every minute."

He had the distinct pleasure of seeing a delicate shade of rose blossom on her cheeks. When she spoke, however, she sounded about as warm as the telephone recording that stated the time. "Do you run a record company, then?"

"No. I own a promotions firm. We bring different acts into town—everything from Pavarotti to Willie Nelson. Rock 'n' roll mostly. We handle the negotiations between agent and arena—arrange for caterers, hotels, the lot. All for an outrageous percentage, of course."

Her lips lifted in an enchanting smile. "It sounds fast-paced . . . and fascinating."

Leaning toward her, he was about to launch into an elaboration when the wine appeared. After sampling the red liquid, Cameron nodded to the waitress, and indicated he would serve the wine himself. Then he began to tilt the bottle toward her glass.

"Oh, none for me, thank you," she said quickly.

"You can't expect me to celebrate alone. Just one glass. It's only Lambrusco," he said firmly as he began pouring.

Her eyes moved from the wine to his face with equal wariness of both. "Are you always so determined to have your own way, Mr. Stone?"

"Cam," he returned instantly. As he righted the bottle his eyes met hers over the glasses, and he noticed how her eyes drooped at the ends. He sat very still, fascinated by their downward turn. The waitress came up with their plates, saving him from having to admit that he'd forgotten what she asked him.

They discussed her suggestions for the apartment. Cam watched her eat, watched the precise little bites she took in between speaking. Her neatness irritated him. He wanted very much to see her rumpled, ruffled, manhandled. It disturbed him because he couldn't understand why he wanted it so much. She had none of the qualities he usually sought in a woman: the outgoing, carefree, ready-for-a-good-time brand of femininity he liked was definitely not part of this lady's repertoire.

Occasionally Julia would take a small cautious sip of wine.

When he finally demanded gruffly to know if she didn't like it, she blinked at him.

"I like it very much. I've always liked Lambrusco," she explained. "It happens to be my favorite brand too." As if to please him, she picked up her glass and emptied it in a swallow.

She set her glass down with a thump, then dared him with a flick of her lashes. He raised his glass in a silent toast to her, then he, too, downed his wine in one gulp. He refilled both glasses and asked her again about colors for the living room. She began to reply, and the conversation was suddenly full, lively. He'd finally succeeded in recharging the electric excitement hidden within her. Their plates were taken away; they didn't notice. A second bottle of wine followed the first, and this time Julia asked to pour, sloshing a bit as she did so.

He wasn't quite certain just when the idea came to him. Maybe it had been there all along, simmering beneath the conscious part of his mind. It erupted full force when, after Julia had filled his glass, he'd proposed a toast to the hope that she'd be called by the realtor very soon. Sips had long since given way to gulps. Julia very carefully set her glass on the wine-spattered table, looked him straight in the eye, and hiccuped.

"Oh!" she exclaimed, her hand flying to cover her mouth. "I *am* sorry." Dismay filled the large blue eyes, and Cam knew without a doubt that he wanted her. He leaned forward.

"Do you want to live in that apartment on the Drive, Julia?"

She nodded and picked up her glass.

"Move in with me."

Her glass was lowered very slowly. Then, just as slowly, Julia began to rise from her seat. His hand flew out to jerk on her wrist.

"What are you doing?" he hissed.

"Thank you for the lunch, Mr. Stone. I shall not, however, thank you for the insult," she stated, snipping each word.

"Will you sit down? I'm not proposing anything like that!" he returned on a fierce whisper.

She hesitated. "You're not?"

"No! Now, sit down and listen."

She sat. He grimaced and released her wrist.

"I have in mind an . . . arrangement," said Cam, watching her closely. He felt ready to tackle her bodily should she again try to leave.

"What sort of arrangement?" she demanded.

He leaned back in his chair, relaxing, now that he had her curious. "You'd probably get a roommate to live with you if you got a place like that, wouldn't you?"

"Yes, but—"

"Why not me?" He pulled out his friendliest there's-nothing-to-worry-about smile. "As you pointed out, it's really too large a place for one, and there's plenty of room for the two of us to live our own lives."

"You can't be serious!" she protested.

He reached for another roll from the basket, and without thinking, Julia handed him the butter. He smiled. "But I am. We'd be strictly roommates. You might find it . . . convenient. I could fend off unwanted men for you."

She watched him sink his teeth into the bread, and she chewed on her lower lip. "But what about you? Wouldn't having a live-in female be rather daunting to your social life?"

"Why should it be? As I said, we'd be strictly roommates."

He saw those big blue eyes slowly inspect him, watched the glass come up against her lips, observed the glistened imprint it left on them when she at last lowered it. All the while he hoped she didn't suspect he was lying through his teeth.

"Beyond that, you could help to discourage the women I don't want bothering me," he added, tapping a fingernail on the table.

"Tell me, do you often have to . . . discourage women?" she asked with quiet interest.

"All the time. In my business—"

"You do?" she interrupted in surprise.

He felt irritation shoot through him. "You may think that

amazing, but other women find me attractive enough," he said in a crisp, cold voice. Her head bent, her blond hair fell forward, and he had the awful suspicion she was stifling a laugh. Slamming his glass to the table with a spray of red wine, he snarled, "We'll just forget the whole damn thing!"

Her head flashed up; her eyes filled with dying humor. "Oh, I *am* sorry!"

"That's quite all right," he said in tones that clearly contradicted his words. "I'm so glad to have amused you."

He was jerking into his coat, but froze as three fingers were placed lightly upon his hand. "Don't go yet," she said softly. Then she withdrew her touch, and Cameron dropped the sleeve of his coat.

"It was a crazy idea anyway," he muttered.

"No," she said. "No, it wasn't crazy. Just . . . unexpected, that's all. I'd like to consider it, if you still would."

"I would," he said emphatically, relaxing a bit.

Then she surprised him by sitting very upright, folding her hands together, and gazing at them with composure. Yes, he thought again, she'd have made a terrific nun.

He sipped his wine and studied the streaks of gold mingling with the darker strands of amber in her hair. He reflected upon the softness of it, imagined sifting his fingers through it.

She raised her head, met his gaze directly, and took a breath. "We'd be just—just roommates? Nothing more?"

"Your opinion of me isn't exactly flattering," he growled, his good mood fading. "I've never had to pressure a woman into anything yet, and I certainly wouldn't start with someone as shapeless as you."

He expected hurt, shock, outrage, some strong reaction to his insult. What he got was laughter. Pure, sparkling, unaffected laughter. When he realized his mouth was agape, Cam brought his lips together with a snap and scowled at her.

Just what the hell was he thinking of anyway? Live with *her*?

He'd sooner live with Vampira. He was going to pay for lunch and get the hell out of there.

He looked down to see a long narrow hand reaching toward him. He looked up to see her smiling at him. He took the hand.

"It's a deal, then, Mr. Stone," she said placidly. After one firm shake she regained her hand. "When do we move in? Do you already have furniture, linens, those sort of things?"

"According to Mrs. O'Neal, I can move in the instant I've signed the lease and made the deposits. I've been living on my own for quite some years now and have all the necessities. What about you?"

"Well, I'm in a furnished apartment now, but I do have linens, plates, pots and pans," she said. "We'll just have to go over everything once we're moved in and unload or store the extras we don't need."

She went into some detail about curtains, rugs, and silverware, until Cameron was forced to interrupt. "I've got to get over and sign the lease, or we won't have any apartment to make plans for. When can you be ready to move in?"

"When can you?" she countered with caution.

Exasperation flickered over his features, but he spoke with decision. "I'll move in this week and get settled in. Then you can move in over the weekend."

They agreed to collect Julia and her things on Sunday afternoon. She didn't ask how or bother him with demands for more or less time. She rose gracefully enough, but stood looking a bit flushed in the face. She stared quite hard at him, then opened her purse. He thought she intended to pay him for her meal, and he began making angry noises. Then he saw she had her laughing eyes fixed on him, and he shut up.

"Here," she said, handing him a card. "Phone me at this number if anything comes up in the meantime. And thank you for lunch."

He watched her skim out of the restaurant, calling himself several interesting and colorful names as she was exiting. Then he looked down at the small white card lodged between his finger and thumb. THE BOOKSHELF, he read, while below that: JULIA HOLLIS, MANAGER. An address was in one corner, a phone number in the other. He knew she had just given him his out. If he changed his mind, he was to call before Sunday, and she'd understand. Well, he'd be damned if he would change his mind!

CHAPTER TWO

Mary Beth Farrow pursed her full lips and gave vent to a shrill whistle.

"I do believe I've seen everything now," she said.

"Don't," stated Julia in a voice of death, "rub it in." Seeing Mary Beth's mouth pucker, she added roughly. "And don't you dare whistle again."

With a ringing laugh that made Julia wince, the short, curvy figure spun away, only to reappear a moment later. She held out her small hand. "Here," she said as she dropped two aspirins into Julia's palm. "Tell me, how did you ever get to be all of twenty-seven without ever before having a hangover? Better yet, tell me how you got one now."

Julia obediently swallowed the aspirins, drank the water held out to her, then sighed. "I'm not too sure. It was just the way he was looking at me—half irritated, half interested. I wanted to shock him, I guess. After downing that first glass in one gulp, the rest slid down like toboggans on a hill."

"I want all the juicy details," said Mary Beth with a wry smile. "But wait a minute." She was gone again in a flash.

Julia could hear a banging in the kitchenette, but kept her eyes firmly shut. If she didn't open them for a long, long time, perhaps when she did, she'd find that the afternoon had all been a dream. She couldn't believe she'd got drunk in the middle of a workday—much less accepted an invitation to move in with a stranger. A male stranger.

She'd known she should refuse when he first said he'd take her to lunch. His tone had suggested he was conferring an honor upon her; in her annoyance she'd decided to go straight back to the bookstore. Then he flashed that unexpected to-hell-with-you look, and she'd found herself agreeing like an idiot. And look where it had landed her. On Mary Beth's lumpy old couch with a pounding head and mouthful of yuck.

"This should help," pronounced Mary Beth, plunking a cold object solidly on top of Julia's blond head. "Ice bag," she explained to the surprise in her friend's face. "Just sit still and let it soothe, then when you're ready, start talking. I'll be here, believe me. I'm not going anywhere till you come clean."

Julie closed her eyes again. She knew full well that behind M.B.'s cheery freckles lay an unshakable tenacity. She managed a weak smile. "Thanks."

Behind her dropped lids she could see a pair of glittering brown eyes giving her the once-over, a pair of squared lips promising passion. Julia forced the image out. Instead, she pictured M.B.'s round face filled with shock when she'd walked into the shop, disheveled and, she was sure, wild-eyed.

She'd had sense enough to leave her car parked at the realtor's, taking the bus back to the Bookshelf on Rush Street. Not that she'd been fit to do a thing once she'd got there. The chill February air failed to have its usual sobering effect, and Julia had arrived giggling. Thinking about it now, she was thankful she hadn't given way to the giggles at the restaurant. The hiccup had been bad enough. She'd seen something dark and exciting flash through his eyes when she'd hiccuped.

Shoving that thought away, she opened her eyes. "What time is it, M.B?"

"Time to talk," was the firm reply. "Actually it's a little past eight. You slept like the proverbial babe from the time I dumped you on the couch somewhere in the vicinity of four. We've got about forty-five minutes till Greg closes up the shop."

"Has Greg been minding the bookstore?"

"All afternoon, ever since he collected your car. Use of husband, however, extends only to the store," she added with a twinkle of mischief. Julia, however, was too miserable to come through with her usual blush.

She made the effort to sit up straight, one hand clamping the ice bag to her crown. She groaned, then grimaced at herself. "Thanks for taking me so well in hand. I don't even remember you bringing me here from the shop. . . ."

"What *do* you remember?" prompted Mary Beth, legs and arms slung carelessly over the colorless armchair that matched the sofa both in the number and variety of lumps.

"Well, I remember going to the realtor's," she began carefully. She recited the bald facts. She made no mention of the way Cameron Stone had gazed at her, the way she'd felt scalded by his look. When she described the lunch, Julia pulled the ice bag from her head and buried her face in it. Jerking it away, she said tonelessly, "And then he suggested we take the apartment together, and I agreed."

Mary Beth leaped from the chair like a spark from a fire. "What? You did *what*?"

"I think—no, I'm sure—I agreed to move in with him," she confessed flatly.

"When? I don't believe it! When, Julie?" shrieked M.B., hopping around her on one foot.

"Sunday. He's to come get me Sunday. If he doesn't change his mind. I gave him one of my cards."

"Well, I'll be damned," said Mary Beth, sinking back into her chair. She shook her frizzy black curls vigorously. "Anyone else, I'd believe—but *you*, you I don't believe. Start at the top, Julie. What did this guy do, slip Love Potion Number Nine in your wine?"

"Oh, it's not *that* kind of arrangement. After all, we're strangers. We're simply going to be roommates. That's it and nothing more," declared Julie with an emphatic nod that shot a pain through her brow. She ignored it to respond to Mary Beth's blatantly skeptical look. "As he pointed out, I'd have gotten a roomie in any case, so why not share it with him?"

"Hmmm," murmured M.B. A line dented her forehead between the two black brows. She looked Julia up and down. She sighed. "And you fell for it. Just what do you suppose is his motivation?"

"What?" Julie's head wasn't in any condition to keep up with M.B.'s reasoning.

"What's his motive? What's this guy getting out of this 'arrangement' if not your scrumptious little bod, hmmm?"

"He says I'll provide him with an excuse to get out of relationships he doesn't want. I'll discourage women from chasing after him."

"Oh? You didn't mention he was so darn sexy."

Julia lowered the ice bag and stared off into the center of M.B.'s tiny living room. "Well, he wasn't Robert Redford. But he did have a sort of . . . appeal."

Mary Beth watched her slippered foot begin swinging beneath the cuff of her blue jeans and waited. After a time, almost as if speaking to herself, Julia continued.

"I guess most people would say he's handsome. He's got the dark good looks that so many women like. . . . His hair was dark brown, thick, and very straight. His eyes were even a deeper brown. He's above medium height. Body well-muscled. Not slim—but definitely not heavy. In shape. He looked confident, used to having his way." She made a face. "But no, I didn't think he was oozing with sex appeal."

"Maybe he's Svengali and you're under his spell," suggested Mary Beth.

"Not likely. I learned to avoid that kind of spell long ago." A certain harshness crept into her voice, then she frowned and said more briskly, "No, I think it was just an impulsive offer—and an impulsive acceptance."

"Would you like some coffee?" Mary Beth jumped up and whisked to the kitchen. A minute later she leaned in the frame of the arch separating the living cubicle from the kitchen cubicle and inquired, "So who is this guy?"

"His name is Cameron Stone and he—" Julia broke off to stare at the recognition fleeting across M.B.'s face. "What's wrong?"

Mary Beth shook her frizzed curls. "I know that name. I know I know that name." She slid her eyes over Julie. "Who is he?"

"Who? I just told you, his name is—"

"No," cut in M.B. impatiently. "I mean, do you know anything else about him? Who he is, what he does?"

"How could I?" returned Julie irritably. "We just met—we're strangers. . . ."

Her reply drifted into empty air. Mary Beth had wheeled back into the kitchenette. Julia could hear muffled curses over the heavy rustling of paper. A triumphant grunt preceded M.B.'s return. She dumped a hastily folded newspaper on Julie's lap. "I knew I knew that name! Read this," she directed, jabbing her finger at the newsprint.

The article beneath M.B.'s stubby finger described a charitable dinner as "the social highlight of the season." The sensually squared features of Cameron Stone jumped out at Julia from one of the grayish photos accompanying the text. The caption read: APPLAUSE FOR CAMERON STONE, PRESIDENT OF STONECO PRODUCTIONS, WHICH HANDLED THE EVENT. Julia glanced at the admiring faces of the women flanking either side of him and slowly lowered the page to gaze blankly into space.

At the sound of a piercing whistle Mary Beth whirled, then came out minutes later carrying two steaming mugs. She handed one to Julie, then sipped from the other, shaking her dark curls at her friend. "One of the city's most eligible bachelors and *you* don't think he's sexy," she said. Her voice fully conveyed her belief that Julia wasn't rowing with both oars.

"Most eligible bachelor?" repeated Julia, nearly spilling her coffee. "What do you mean?"

"That's what the papers call him. He must be something of a playboy. He's in the society pages just about every week. The line of women he's squired about town probably stretches to New York."

The mug sat neglected in her hand as Julia soaked in this information. It was not, on the whole, pleasant reflection. She wasn't given to impulsive action. Her life was carefully controlled, meticulously planned. She'd made one mistake and had vowed never to fall into an emotional trap again. Now it seemed she'd picked up a loaded pistol and begun a game of Russian roulette. And as much as she'd like to blame it on the Lambrusco, Julie had the sinking feeling that a pair of liquid brown eyes had been responsible for her agreement to move in with Cameron Stone.

The banging on the apartment door startled her. She looked up to see Greg grinning at her. It was a fact of life that if Greg Farrow smiled at you, you returned it, no matter how glum your mood. She reluctantly grinned back.

"Thanks for taking over the store," she said as he settled himself on the arm of his wife's chair. "Did you have to cut any classes to do it?"

"Not a one," he answered with a tinge of regret. "But if you want to get looped tomorrow, there's Winn's class at two. . . ."

Freckles flew in all directions as he grinned more broadly than ever. Julia laughed, then immediately sighed and plopped the ice bag back on her head.

Sliding naturally into the curve of Greg's arm, Mary Beth extended a finger and pushed his wire-rim glasses firmly up the bridge of his nose. "You aren't going to believe what our prim and proper Miss Hollis has done."

"Oh? There's more?" he asked with a laugh that was full of love. He rumpled the tight mop of black curls so very like his own, and as so often happened when she was with them, Julie felt a surge of envy at their obvious happiness together.

She couldn't imagine a more perfect couple. They even looked alike, except that where M.B. was all curves, Greg was all angles.

Both had friendly freckled faces topped with dark dancing curls and smiles that reflected their joy in life, in one another. Looking at them now, Julia gave vent to another sigh, this one from an inner pain no amount of aspirin or ice could remedy.

"If I gave you an entire lifetime to guess, you wouldn't," Mary Beth said knowingly, "so I'm going to tell you. Julie agreed to move into that apartment today."

He looked down into the teasing face of his wife. "So?"

"So . . . she's got a roommate," she said, drawing it out. Julia closed her eyes. "A roommate of the male gender. A playboy named Cameron Stone, in fact," finished Mary Beth with all the satisfaction of one who's delivered the goods.

There was a prolonged silence. Julie was forced to reopen her eyes. Greg's glinted back at her, magnified by the lenses of his glasses. "Was this before or after the wine?" he inquired dryly.

Mary Beth snorted. "What do you think? And *she* doesn't seem to believe he could have ulterior motives!" A second snort underscored her opinion of such feeble reasoning.

Julia attempted a wavering smile. "It's not that kind of arrangement. We hardly know each another, after all. We'd just be roommates, nothing more."

Her argument sounded forced. Greg looked clearly skeptical. He rose with his usual gangly movement. The lady doth protest too much, thought Julia as she removed the ice bag once again, setting it onto the upturned wooden crate that served as an end table.

"Do you mean to go ahead with it, Julie?" he asked.

Julia thought about the way Cameron's eyes went black as they worked their way over her. She thought about how her nerves had danced when he grabbed her arm. She thought about the delightful warm buzz at lunch. But that, she quickly reminded herself, had been the Lambrusco.

"I . . . don't know," she replied hesitantly. She rubbed her temples with both hands and stared at her crumpled wool skirt. "My mother would probably faint."

"Oh, your mother!" exclaimed Mary Beth in disgust. "She's in South Dakota, for Pete's sake! How would she even know?"

"I wasn't being literal," sighed Julia. "It's—oh, I don't know! —it's the guilt I'd feel just knowing how she'd feel if she *did* know. You may think this is almost the twenty-first century, but where I come from, it's still the Ice Age. Divorce still has the power to shock in my hometown. Can you imagine what living with a man would do?"

"At your age, Julie, you should be living for yourself, not for your mother," insisted Mary Beth. "But don't get me wrong. I think you'd be crazy to move in with a man who seems to change women as often as Greg changes socks. But it's past time for you to quit being repressed by that small-town upbringing of yours."

"Come on, let's get some food," said Greg, nudging M.B. toward the kitchen. "We'll all think better on full stomachs."

He followed her out, leaving Julia alone to meditate. She listened to the rattle of pots and pans, the banging of cupboard doors, the murmur of voices and knew Greg and Mary Beth were talking about her. She knew any major decisions on her part would be examined and discussed and assessed by them. From the day Julia hired Mary Beth as a clerk at the bookstore, she'd been irrevocably adopted by the Farrows. Though the pair were several years younger than she, their attitude toward her was parental and deeply caring. She returned their affection in full measure, but wasn't always able to stifle a certain melancholy she felt when with them. They were so very happy together—a type of happiness that seemed destined to elude her.

Over dinner not another word was said about Julia's afternoon, due, she suspected, to stern lecturing from Greg to his madcap wife. They focused instead on Greg's classes at Northwestern, where he was working toward a graduate degree in computer science. Neither seemed to mind that their inattentive guest only joined the conversation spasmodically. After finishing the ground-beef casserole and helping to clean up, Julia left, steadfastly declining their offer to see her home.

It wasn't until she'd changed into her flannel nightgown and crawled beneath the blankets on her narrow twin bed that Julia permitted herself to face the image that had been nagging at her ever since she woke up on M.B.'s sofa. It loomed up in the shadows of her apartment and mocked her relentlessly.

Allen.

The name still had the power to hurt her. She wondered who'd ever said . . . Out of sight, out of mind. It simply wasn't true. No one knew better than she how a memory could expand—filling the mind and blocking out all other images. The memory of Allen took control now, and Julia tossed restlessly in its grip.

Grams always said she was a late bloomer, that she had awakened slowly to the realities of life around her. Sheltered and introspective, Julie was a loner even as a child, preferring the company of hollyhocks and moonbeams to that of people. She grew up entertaining herself, fantasizing—through books—about special worlds that relied on no one else for her happiness. In high school, still wrapped within her private dreams, she hadn't shared her friends' all-consuming interest in boys; she'd dated only intermittently. The pattern lasted long after she'd begun college. She lived at home, where it was easy to remain the "child" Grams still called her, postponing the responsibilities of being a woman.

After graduating from her tiny hometown college, Julia enrolled at Northwestern University to get a master's degree in library science. At twenty-two she'd finally made the adventurous leap into life on her own. From the first she'd liked Chicago. She liked the myriad congestion of people crowding the city, the clamorous rumblings of the elevated trains squealing around the Loop, the colorful outsize sculptures decorating the downtown streets. She liked the exhilarating collection of dirt and color and noise that made Chicago pulse with life. She'd stepped from the plane at O'Hare knowing life would never be the same again.

Precisely one month later she met Allen Kessler.

She'd had no warning before he'd collided into her as she was hurriedly crossing the campus. She remembered how he'd scattered books and papers over concrete and grass. It'd been, she now thought, highly symbolic of the way he crashed into her life, shattering her heart. Brilliantly handsome, as golden as a shining sun, he was totally unlike any other male she had ever known. He disarmed her with continual whimsy: words of love stamped into the snow outside her apartment window, poems delivered to her door with a pizza, flower petals showered over her textbooks. He charmed her into love and eventually into his bed.

Her mind awhirl with memories, Julia gave up trying to sleep and sat up, drawing her knees up to her chin. In the mooncast glimmers of the night she could almost imagine the glow of Allen's blond hair as she'd seen it so many times upon her pillow. Would she ever stop yearning for him?

It wasn't even as if they'd lived together. A sophomore when they met, Allen kept his dorm room at the college, staying over at Julia's only on occasional weekends. To be near him she remained in Chicago after getting her graduate degree, eventually taking the position of manager at the Bookshelf. Though not pleased, her parents had been resigned to the fact that a woman of twenty-four must know her own mind.

Her heavy sigh split the night. If only she had! Or, to be more precise, if only she'd known Allen's mind. *She* had known they would be married, but quelled her impatience, knowing it was necessary for him first to get his degree. When the day of his graduation came, no cloud of premonition darkened her sunny skies. It wasn't until three weeks later that the thunderheads rolled in.

Allen abruptly announced his acceptance of a job in San Francisco. He said he was sorry it didn't work out, but he thanked Julie for what he called "all the good times" and left the next day.

It was a trite story. It happened to thousands of women every day, women who went on with their lives. Julia often wondered why she'd been unable to recover. After two years she still bruised at the thought of him. Oh, she'd seen other men, mostly out of pride and boredom. But in an era where men expected more from their dates than the conventional good-night kiss, Julie's fear of involvement without total commitment soon earned her the reputation of being frigid. In recent months she'd had fewer and fewer dates and that, she said fiercely to the darkness, was just the way she wanted to keep it!

How could she have been so foolish as to agree to share an apartment with a strange man? And, from what M.B. had said, a playboy at that! The last thing she wanted was to get involved —however platonically—with another heartbreaker.

She stretched out once more and forced herself to relax. She had no doubt that Cameron Stone would be calling to laugh over how silly wine could make you.

By the time Julia let herself into the bookshop on Friday morning, she was beginning to wonder if Cameron had indeed been serious. She'd halfheartedly started packing up her dishes and clothes, telling herself all the while how ridiculous it was. She knew she ought to forget the whole insane idea. But she couldn't quite seem to do it. Something in her yearned for the opportunity to change her life, to experience something new.

The aroma of mellowed paper and musty leather soothed her, as it always did. Old books were, to her, old and dear friends. She walked past shelves crowded to the ceiling, past tables and glass cases artlessly arranged, letting the quiet warmth seep into her soul.

The Bookshelf was a secondhand store, dealing in used volumes, from the rare antique to the classic novel. Even the shop itself was an antique. Housed in a block of old buildings that had somehow escaped the Great Fire, the Bookshelf had an old wooden floor that sloped; small steps ran up or down in unexpected places, and the stairs to the concrete basement were rickety. Alcoves with stools or benches for the serious browser added to the drowsy atmosphere. Julia loved every square inch of it, every book in it, with all the emotion she denied to people.

At the back of the store was a glass counter. A series of steps to the left led to the manager's office. Julia entered the office, shrugged out of her coat, stuffed her suede gloves into the pockets, and hung it on a hook by the door. She measured coffee granules, poured water into the coffeemaker, then turned to her desk just as the phone pealed, shattering the quiet.

"The Bookshelf. Good morning," she said rather absently as she looked over notecards sprinkling her desk.

"Miss Hollis?"

Julia's breath caught, then she forced out a word: "Yes?"

"Cameron Stone."

"Yes," she repeated. A sense of disappointment assailed her. Don't be a fool, she told herself. Be grateful that he, at least, has come to his senses.

"I . . . that is—" he began. She could hear an impatient tapping, a restless unseen message. Then a draft of breath. "Have you changed your mind?"

"Have you?" she returned with a composure she did not feel.

"Do you always answer questions with questions?" he asked rather sharply.

"Do you?" She thought she heard a smothered curse. Carefully hiding her thoughts, she said softly, "I quite understand, Mr. Stone. Let's say we blame it on the Lambrusco and let it go at that."

"Ahhh," he said, drawing it out into a long sigh. "So you have changed your mind."

"Not at all," she disclaimed instantly. "But as it is, after all, your signature on the lease, I believe you should have the last word on this—arrangement of ours."

As the silence stretched out, with only the heavy rapping to sound in her ear, Julia admonished herself. A simple yes would have ended the entire matter and she hadn't come close to saying it. If Nobel prizes were given out for stupidity, she'd have just walked off with the award. Suddenly she realized the tapping had stopped.

"Mr. Stone?" she inquired tentatively.

"I don't know where the hell you live. If I'm to pick you up on Sunday, it would be nice to know where I'm going."

The sarcasm was lost on her. All Julie's attention was given to the curious fluttering of her heart, to the odd sensation of having run several blocks. Calling on long practice, she forced herself to respond levelly.

"It isn't actually necessary for you to come get me, Mr. Stone —"

"Cam. If we're sharing an apartment, we should at least be on a first-name basis," he said with a touch of humor in his voice. He sounded more relaxed, and hearing it, Julie relaxed too.

"Of course. I have my own car, Cam, and I can easily pack my few worldly goods into it. I'll drive myself over at, say, one?" Her hand crept up to play nervously with her hair. Julie was glad he couldn't see her, for she very much feared she was blushing.

"Sounds good. Are you sure you don't need help with the packing, Julia?"

"No, but thank you."

"Well, that's that, then. I'll see you on Sunday at one."

"Yes." She had the insane notion that he could feel the butterflies leaping in her midsection. There was a pause. She wondered why he didn't say good-bye and hang up.

"I think we should try to get better acquainted," he said at last. "I'll pick you up for dinner tonight at seven."

His cool assumption that she'd agree stunned her. Hearing his breathing punctuate her astonished silence, Julie told herself to snap out of it. "No," she stated simply.

"What?" he asked.

"No. I said no, Cam. This isn't going to be that kind of relationship. If you think it is, then we'd best call a halt to the whole idea right now."

"I'm only talking dinner, for Christ's sake," he said harshly.

"I don't want anything else any more than you do. But I thought we should talk a bit more before Sunday."

"Would it change your mind?" Her voice sounded as if it were coated with an inch of ice.

"No, dammit, I just—"

"Then I'm sorry, but I don't see the point in any dates—dinner or otherwise—between us. We'll get to know each other soon enough once we're settled in the apartment."

"All right, have it your way."

The phone slammed in her ear with a marked degree of anger. Julia felt oddly thrilled, as if she'd won a skirmish in the battle of the sexes. She was humming when the buzzer on the front door sounded. Running lightly down the steps, she pressed the button under the counter that released the lock on the door and allowed M.B. to push her way in. She grinned widely at her friend, feeling that this was truly a beautiful morning, and ignored the raised black brows and the questioning eye.

"What's with you, huh? You look like the cat that just ate the canary." Mary Beth pulled off her metallic ski jacket and mittens as she took in Julia's glittering blue eyes, the flushed cheeks, the curving lips.

"Oh, nothing really," said Julie airily. "Cameron Stone just called."

"And you call that nothing!" With a shake of her head Mary Beth went into the office, hung up her jacket, and poured two cups of coffee. She returned, handing one to Julie, then asked offhandedly, "So what gives?"

"I'm moving over on Sunday."

"Are you sure about this, Julie?"

"No," she answered simply. Julia watched the struggle reflected in M.B.'s round face and heard her heavy sigh.

"Well, God knows, you need a change in your life, but I can't help worrying this one may be too much all at once. Julie, this guy moves in the fast lane with a speedy set!"

"There's no sense in worrying before any damage is done. So

far all I'm losing is a half month's rent and a five-year-old deposit on my apartment." After a sip of coffee she added thoughtfully, "But you're right. I do need a change. Perhaps that's why I accepted the idea in the first place. I can count on the fingers of one hand the people I currently socialize with. My last date was well over three months ago and *that* was a less-than-thrilling evening of bowling. . . . My life's become absolutely routine, M.B., each day a repetition of the day before. Even if it doesn't work out, I'll at least be getting out of the rut I've been in the last two years."

The buzzer sounded the arrival of the day's first customer. As Mary Beth moved toward the button she threw over her shoulder, "Did you say getting out of your rut? I'd say you're blowing it up with a ton of TNT!"

CHAPTER THREE

She was packed and ready to go by nine o'clock on Sunday morning. Mary Beth and Greg had shown up the night before, bearing a pizza and an offer of help. They'd finished her packing in a flurry of laughter that seemed to echo in Julie's mind as she wandered listlessly through the small apartment that had never been more than a stopping place. When noon finally arrived, she took her keys to the apartment manager's office and said good-bye. Then she got in her dented sky-blue Toyota and drove aimlessly along Lake Shore Drive, beyond Lincoln Park, before turning back toward her destination.

As she drove she had the odd sensation that a hand was gripping the base of her throat, choking the breath from her lungs. She barely noticed the shimmer of Lake Michigan through the trees that had been stripped for winter. Her mind was occupied with warnings about not making a fool of herself. The last thing in the world she wanted was to betray her agitation to Cameron Stone. He was certain to misinterpret it. Although she truly believed that she needed a change in her life, she didn't want a personal involvement.

She'd have been relieved to know that no hint of her inner turmoil was visible in the composure she displayed as she parked before the tall brick building that was her new home. The front door opened as she got out. Moving to the rusted rear of her car, she hid her incredible awareness of his approach. By the time she had her trunk open, Cam was at her side. Out of the corner of her eye she could see the pine-green sweater stretching over his chest, the faded blue jeans riding low on his hips.

She'd told M.B. he wasn't sexy. And really she'd *thought* he wasn't. Faced with the reality of him now, however, she had to revise her opinion.

It wasn't so much his dark good looks—though she had to admit, he was far more attractive than she'd remembered. It was the way he carried himself. He walked with an air of assurance, almost boldness; obviously he was a man confidently pleased with the niche he'd carved in life. And perhaps it was the way his eyes brightened with the reflected splinters of his smile. Julia quickly clamped down on her errant thoughts.

"You're right on time," he said, his voice warm and friendly. He felt an unwarranted amount of pleasure at the sight of her blue jeans beneath her long coat. They made her seem more human, more accessible. "It's just one o'clock."

"Yes," she said, and wondered why his smile had vanished.

He bent and wordlessly lifted the biggest box out of her trunk then carried it on into the apartment. With a shrug Julie picked up another and followed him.

Cameron kicked open the unlocked door with a violence completely out of proportion to the situation. The instant she'd spoken that brief hushed affirmative, he'd begun to regret the whole thing. She wasn't as pretty as he'd remembered, Cameron mused, and his disappointment rankled. What the hell had he been thinking? She was about as animated as a lamppost! He must have been drunk to ever imagine making love to her.

Setting the box on the carpet, he turned to go get another one, then halted abruptly. Julia stood in the threshold, her arms wrapped tightly around cardboard, her eyes wide with surprise as she took in the living room.

"Oh, Cameron," she breathed in a voice that totally erased his hostility. She lowered the box and moved into the room.

"You like it?" he asked casually.

Her eyes slowly swept over the flowered Chinese blue wingback chairs standing on one side of the fireplace, the matching sofa on the other, and past the rosewood side table to rest on the window niche. A plumply cushioned couch of deep cobalt hugged all three walls. Plants hung in varying lengths from the windows. Massive upended stereo speakers acted as tables.

"Oh, Cam," she repeated.

Turning to face him, Julia focused a blinding smile upon him. *This* was the Julia he'd thought about all week! The dazzling, vibrant Julia that he wanted. Just as he was feeling his first stirrings of heat, she spun away from him, racing lightly through the apartment. He waited, listening to doors open and shut with a smile of satisfaction. Twice he heard the clap of her hands, which he recognized as a signal of her excitement. On a mental scoreboard he'd just knocked in a home run.

She returned slowly, taking each step as if she'd just discovered how to walk. A peach glow of pleasure suffused her delicate features.

"How?" she asked. "How on earth did you manage to accomplish all this in one week?"

"Ve haff our vays," he bantered, teasing her with his eyes as he spoke. The glow on her cheeks deepened, pleasing him. He cocked a dark brow. "You see, I did listen to your suggestions at lunch."

Julia's first rush of pleasure at seeing the apartment as she'd envisioned it gave way to a barrage of doubts. Her gaze retraced the furnishings in the living room. They were of superior quality, as they'd been in every other room. And unmistakably new. What kind of man could command that such an enormous job of decorating be done in under a week? The cost alone . . .

"This must have cost you a fortune," she finally said.

He shrugged. *A man who shrugs away a fortune,* she thought with dismay.

"Don't worry about it. If you like what's been done, then it's well worth it" was all he said before he went out to finish unloading her car.

It took Julia several seconds to follow him. Fresh doubts assailed her. Did he expect something more out of their arrangement? His tone had been more suggestive than a line from a Mae West movie, his smooth appraisal equally provocative. And, she mused with a frown, a darn sight too assured! She had to make it clear to him that theirs would be a straightforward sharing of the apartment, nothing more. Ever.

With her face once more an impassive mask, she joined Cam outside to help finish unloading the trunk and both seats of the car. While he moved the now empty car to the tenant carports behind the building, Julie hung her coat in the closet and tucked her straw-colored shirt into her jeans. Knowing how vivid colors, particularly blues, accentuated her elusive beauty, she'd long ago pared her wardrobe to only the most neutral shades. She didn't think of her clothes now, however, but of Cam Stone.

The man breathed a sensual charm the way most people breathed air, she thought. It made Julia feel uneasy. That much disturbing attraction had a hollow ring. She wouldn't trust Cameron as far as the corner. But she couldn't deny the appeal of his lopsided smile or his warm dark eyes. It had been, she finally admitted, that very attraction that had led to her impulsive acceptance of this dangerous arrangement.

How, she demanded of herself with a heavy sigh, could she have been so softheaded? It was rather like lighting a match near an open can of gasoline. Now she had to do what she could to make certain it didn't explode. She would ignore that charm of his, Julia decided. After all, she wasn't stupid enough to fall for a superficial charmer twice in the same lifetime!

Cam's appeal was much in evidence when he reentered. He was whistling under his breath and smiling at her with those incredible brown eyes. He stopped in front of the pile amassed in the living room. "Is this really everything you own?" he inquired, voice filled with disbelief.

Six cardboard boxes, two labeled KITCHEN, two marked BOOKS, one LINENS and one BATH, plus two suitcases and a nightcase. Over the arm of the sofa draped a jumble of clothes on hangers. Cameron took stock of her "worldly goods," as she had called them, then raised his eyes to study her. He'd always believed women were more materialistic, more apt to collect possessions, than a man, perhaps because of a homemaking instinct. If that were true, it was an instinct Julia Hollis clearly lacked.

"How old are you?" he asked.

She stared at him, realizing how easily she could annoy him by not answering. "Twenty-seven," she responded at last. Before he could probe further, she lifted a kitchen box and started down the hall.

With so little to unpack the chore was completed well before dusk. Julia had been given the back bedroom, near the kitchen, and she was delighted with the simple, straight-lined oak furniture Cam had chosen. She sat on the queen-size bed and ran her hand lingeringly over the soft velveteen blanket. Her linens box now stood at the back of her closet, unopened. Twin sheets and blankets were of little use on a bed this size. She would discard them without regret, accepting with pleasure the linens Cam had selected to replace them.

The thought shook her. How could this *stranger* understand what she would or would not like? She stared at the delicate roses splayed over the cream pillowcases. She tried to imagine Cameron purchasing the lovely sheets. Instead of amusing her, the image careened through her mind with frightening intensity.

More than ever she understood why Cam had suggested she move in with him. Looking at the fine furnishings in this room alone, it was obvious he had more than enough money for the rent; he didn't need a roommate. Well, if he had her marked down as bed warmer, he was in for a shock!

She moved to the dresser, took up her purse, and extracted a small black notebook and pen from its depths. In a neat flowing hand she compiled a list of what she owed Mr. Stone to date. Item: set of queen-size sheets. Item: two queen-size blankets—

one pink thermal-weave, one buff velveteen. Item: phone installation. Item: utility hookup. Item: groceries. Item: rent.

When she had a long row of such items, Julia tore the sheet from her notebook and replaced the book in her purse. She folded her list and stuck it in the back pocket of her jeans, then set off in search of her roommate.

The first of the front bedrooms was now a family room of sorts with Hide-A-Bed sofa, desk, and television set. Louvered doors, painted the same high-gloss white as the moldings, hid a wall of shelves where Cam had installed state-of-the-art stereo equipment, a video cassette deck, and other electronic toys. Having left Julia to settle her room to her liking, he now lounged on the sofa, half watching a sports show on the set.

The other half of him was wishing he knew what to say to Julia. This was an unusual problem for him. The things he knew to say to women—sometimes with only his eyes, his hands, his lips—definitely could not be said to this woman. She'd posted a HANDS OFF sign in letters a mile high, then reinforced it with that cool dispassion that so unreasonably annoyed him. With her Cam would have to practice a patience that was foreign to him. Again he wondered if she'd be worth the trouble. She puzzled him, she irritated him, and she unaccountably attracted him.

"Shall we talk before or after dinner?" she asked from the doorway, startling him.

"Talk?" he echoed stupidly, pulled from his thoughts with a jolt.

"About our arrangement," she explained. She came in smoothly, almost floating, and sat on the chair before the satinwood desk. "We must have things clear from the start or we'll run straight into trouble."

"I thought we'd already cleared things," returned Cameron, his brows jerking together.

"I'm not speaking about the personal end of our agreement. That has already been made perfectly clear," she stated calmly.

She cast a quick glance at the colorful blur on the television. "We can talk later if you like."

With a near growl of exasperation, Cameron punched a button on his remote control, and the blur disappeared. "Well? Talk."

Folding her hands in her lap, Julie met his scowl without a flinch. But she took a moment to compose her thoughts. She'd just noticed how his squared lips tilted at the edges, and it disconcerted her. She really didn't understand why she was suddenly noticing how his mouth tipped or how very long his eyelashes were or how his straight brows arched in temper. She forced herself to rein in her straying thoughts.

"I think we should define everything at the outset. As roommates, we should split everything fifty-fifty."

"Just what do you mean by everything?"

"Exactly that. Utilities, grocery bills—and housework. Chores should be split as evenly as costs."

He leaned back into the rust corduroy of the couch, one arm flung across the length of the back. "Can everything be split down the middle? Take the groceries, for instance. Would it be fair for you to have to pay half the cost of my beer? Or for me to pay for something you eat, but I don't?"

"What we need and use together, we'd buy at our fifty-fifty rate. Any personal extras we each get on our own expense, and neither dips into the other's specialties without permission."

She was once again wearing what he thought of as her nun's face—placid and serene. Her complacency annoyed him. He wanted very much to prick at it, to make her laugh or yell or in any way reveal some of the spirit he knew she possessed. "You have this all worked out, haven't you?" he queried coolly. "What about other bills?"

"Down the middle. We'd each pay our own long-distance calls, of course, but halve the basic phone charge. As for the housework," she continued in the same sober tone, "I suggest we each maintain our own bedroom and bathroom. The others we can clean together on the weekend. We can alternate cooking meals and doing the dishes."

He started to shake his head, cocoa-colored strands of hair scraping the collar of his sweater. Seeing this, Julie felt a spurt of vexation. "Don't expect that because I'm female, I'm going to take over the burden of cleaning and cooking!"

His brows flew up and his eyes glittered brightly. It was a gleam of—what? Triumph? Julie wasn't certain, but she did realize that her moment of anger somehow had excited him, and she noted to herself not to lose control again.

"Of course not," he said easily, light laughter threading through his tone. "I was about to tell you that I've got a maid."

"You what?"

"I said, I've got a maid." He smiled wickedly. "I might let you have her for your share of the work . . . if the price is right."

Recalling her lesson of a moment ago Julia choked down her rising temper at the suggestion blatantly underscoring his words. She set her features into a blank cast. "If indeed you have a maid service," she said tonelessly, "Then I shall pay half her salary. That leaves the cooking and dishes. Can you cook?"

"Oh, hell!" he expostulated. Her damned impassivity erased his humor, leaving a stinging irritation. He jumped up and strode out before Julie could react.

She heard the banging of cupboard doors as she very slowly walked down the long passage to the kitchen. Nearer she heard the clinking of ice against a glass, the pouring of liquid. When she came in, he glared at her over the rim of a whiskey glass. Julia's eyes met his for one searing instant, then dropped. She felt as if her insides had been detonated.

"Go set the table," he ordered curtly, startling her into looking back up at him.

"What?"

Seeing her bewilderment, Cam's tension eased. "If I'm doing the cooking, shouldn't you be setting the table?"

"*Are* you doing the cooking?" she countered.

"If you'll get out of the kitchen and let me get to work." He set down his glass and tugged off his sweater. Tossing it carelessly onto a nearby counter, he began rolling up his sleeves. He arched his brows at her. "Well?"

She proffered a mock salute and trod down the hall to the china cabinet. Once out of his sight she leaned against the glass doors and held onto the latch to steady herself. She'd been taken by surprise when he removed his sweater and the simple action—the flex of his arms, the intake of his stomach as he pulled—had caught her unawares. Her reaction had been immediate. Her heart was doing the hundred-yard dash, while her stomach was pole-vaulting. His shirt had been unbuttoned at the top and the mere glimpse of his chest had knocked the wind from her.

Her mind seemed to have split in two. One half argued, He's nothing like Allen! Why not take a chance? Why not let yourself enjoy this incredible excitement you feel? The other half shouted back, Okay, so he's not a blond god, and he frowns more than he laughs, but underneath he's just like Allen! Just as shallow, just as ready to dish out pain on top of the pleasure. You can't ignore that I'd-like-to-eat-you-for-dessert gleam in his eyes!

Julie shook herself and sternly commanded both halves to shut up. She opened the cabinet and selected two pieces of her own china—plain white plates with a thin line of silver around the rim—and two woven wheat placemats. Marching to the dining room, she thumped them into place, setting one mat at the head of the polished oak table and, after some deliberation, the other just to the right. When she'd finished setting out glasses, silver, and napkins, she was calm enough to return to the kitchen.

Cam was waiting for her. Handing her a knife and a cucumber, he grinned. "Chop."

Together they prepared a fancy tossed salad, Cam showing Julie how to dice Bermuda onions at a boggling speed. As he flourished his knife a delicious aroma wafted from the oven, and she began to realize he knew his way around the kitchen.

"Don't expect such culinary wonders from me," she warned

as she shredded romaine lettuce into a bowl. "Two ground-beef casseroles and a meat loaf are about all I've ever mastered."

"Don't you know it's said bachelors will eat anything?"

"You haven't tasted my meat loaf," she returned dryly.

She shook her hands, spraying a fine mist as she did so, then reached for a linen towel lying in a heap on the counter. By the time she realized Cam had yelled "Don't!" she'd already pulled on it. A brittle, splintering crash sounded as a hot, greasy liquid spilled over her hand, burning her the instant before she jumped back.

Cam grabbed her arm and turned on the tap in one swift motion. He thrust her hand under the cold water and stood behind her. "Damn, I'm sorry! I should have told you to watch out for that. Are you very badly burned?"

"No, I don't think so," she replied. She was more aware of his heated breath grazing her cheek as he spoke than she was of the stinging of her hand. He pressed against her and she could feel the muscles of his thigh tighten. "What was it?" she asked, more to distract herself than to find out how she'd been burned.

"A small bowl of melted butter. I'd wrapped it in the towel to keep it hot while I diced some garlic cloves to mix with it. . . . For garlic bread," he added as he pulled her hand out from under the stream of water.

She shifted, attempting to step away, but he pushed her into the edge of the sink, his chest rubbing against her back while he examined her hand. "I—it's okay," she said quickly. "Really. I'll go put something on it."

He nodded, seemed to hesitate, then moved slightly back from her. He maintained his hold on her hand and started nudging her toward the hall. "There's some Mycitracin in the medicine cabinet of my bathroom. I'll rub it over your hand and you'll—"

"No!" Julie forcefully pulled her hand free, then hastily covered her agitation with a cool smile. "I can take care of it, Cam. You'd better clean up this mess I made. I'll meet you at the table when I've gotten myself changed." She held up her hand, showing the butter-splattered cuff of her blouse.

With trembling limbs she left him before he could stop her. The burn on her hand was nothing compared to the scalding her nerve endings had just received. This was never going to work if she reacted like a lightning rod in an electrical storm every time Cam got within two feet of her. For the first time since Allen had left her, Julie was trying, really trying, to recall her reactions to him when they'd first met. Had she felt like this? Had she experienced the same shock waves of physical awareness?

She gave up. She'd been too successful blocking out those particular memories to be certain of her recollections now. What she thought she'd felt had become colored by the events that followed. She was certain, however, that her reactions to Cameron Stone were just as dangerous, if not more so, than whatever she'd once felt for Allen Kessler.

Slowly working the ointment into her skin, she looked around Cam's bathroom, noting that he used the same brand of toothpaste she did. But he seemed to squeeze the tube wherever his hand landed. She always rolled neatly from the bottom up to the top. The observation unnerved her further. She didn't want to know how he squeezed his toothpaste! Such intimate knowledge had no place in their relationship. She swiped the excess grease off her hand with a tissue and fairly ran from the room.

Once she'd changed into a plain cream turtleneck, she took a deep breath, reminded herself it was "roommates only," and made her way back to the dining room. Cam was already seated at the head of the table. The mixed greens of the tossed salad showed through a clear glass bowl, while beside it steam wisped tantalizingly from a casserole. An open bottle of red wine caught her eye. It was the same brand of Lambrusco they'd had in the restaurant. Her favorite brand.

"It smells heavenly," she said as she took her seat. "What is it?"

"Lasagna," replied Cam. He leaned forward, reaching out to take her hand in his.

Julie swiftly unfurled the white linen napkin onto her lap, masterfully avoiding the contact with Cam. With a quick sidelong glance she caught his heavy frown.

"How's your hand?" he asked on a near snap.

"Fine."

"Good," he said, sounding rather disappointed she wasn't in agonizing pain. He picked up the bottle and tilted it in her direction. "Wine?"

"Please."

He served them both, then began to eat, looking only at his plate. Suddenly he dropped his fork against the plate with a ping. "Let me see it," he demanded.

Julie held her fork poised above her plate. She looked momentarily confused. "What?"

"Your hand. Let me see your hand, Julia."

It wasn't a request. It was an imperial command. She only thought of defying him for an instant; he was, after all, just showing friendly concern. She held out the burned hand. He didn't touch her, contenting himself with merely eyeing it before leaning back in his chair, satisfied she wasn't seriously hurt.

"This is very good," commented Julie after a lengthy silence. "With the way you can cook, I'm surprised some woman hasn't snapped you up long ago."

His dark gaze slid over her. "I'm very adept at sidestepping the traps women set. There isn't a trick in the book I haven't learned to avoid."

"Is that how you view a relationship? As a trap?" Her voice was utterly void. He couldn't see her left hand knotting the napkin in her lap.

He raised a quizzical brow. "I thought you were referring to marriage."

"I suppose I was, but what difference does it make?"

He laughed, and his voice seemed to melt over her. "There are relationships, and there are relationships."

His suggestive tone annoyed her. She set down her fork and studied his face for several moments before speaking. "Marriage isn't a trap. Or shouldn't be. It's a commitment between two people to make a relationship last."

"Oh, come on. You can't believe that! Have you noticed the divorce rate recently? One in four marriages does *not* last—that should tell you something about commitment, Julia." He took a leisurely sip of his wine, watching her all the while. "You're only committed to someone for as long as the enjoyment lasts."

"Would you ask an employer to hire you only for as long as you were having a good time? A relationship isn't all fun and games. It's responsibility and work too."

She'd bent toward him, speaking emphatically, sincerely. Cam's eyes narrowed at the emotion in her voice, hiding his flash of desire from her. "Oh, I'd work to make a relationship fun," he drawled, enjoying the flush rising in her thin face.

Picking up her fork, Julia attacked her lasagna with savage intent. She had known that would be his attitude! Bitterly she remembered Allen telling her how sorry he was, but, he had said, "The fun had gone out of their relationship."

Cameron kept his eyes on her while he refilled their wine-glasses. Her annoyance pleased him. He'd been absolutely right about her. She was as old-fashioned as she looked. The notion added a certain thrill to the hunt. He'd pierce that cool armor of hers soon enough. He'd make her realize what a great time they could have together.

He began speaking in a casually friendly way. In unspoken agreement they restricted the rest of their conversation to strictly impersonal topics. They discovered a common interest in movies, and a lively debate ensued over the merits of the latest offering from a well-known flamboyant director they both admired. By the end of that discussion they were both surprised to realize they'd finished eating long ago.

"I suppose we'd better clean up," said Cam with a grin.

Julie's heart did a curious flip-flop. "I'll do the washing up. You cooked, I'll clean."

He stood and began gathering dishes together. "You helped fix the salad, remember? We'll both clean up. I'll wash—I don't want you putting hot water on your hand."

He had a way of stating things that left her no room to argue. She collected the empty salad bowl, the wine bottle and coaster, and marched down the hall in his wake.

When they'd briskly finished clearing the table, they went into the study and watched the television with unseeing eyes. Julie sat on the carpet, her back propped against the sofa, and felt distressfully conscious of Cam's presence behind her. She didn't want to be aware of him! Whether he was miles or mere inches away from her should be a matter of supreme indifference. It should be, but somehow Julie couldn't stop listening to the rhythm of his breathing, to the rustle of his jeans whenever he shifted his weight.

Above her, stretched full-length on the couch, Cameron had a more pleasurable distraction. He stared at the blond hair just beyond his hand and counted the varying streaks in it. That strand was definitely sunstruck, Cameron thought; that one, a silvery ash; while this one, the one closest to his fingertip, was a deeper flaxen. It would have been even more pleasurable to touch each strand, but, knowing she was not ready to welcome his caress, he restrained himself.

The evening news came on, and Julie yawned, stretched, and stood. Cam's eyes followed each liquid motion. She rested her hands on her hips, her fingers curling back to the rear of her jeans, and he pictured his own fingers there instead. Suddenly she was straighter, a piece of paper in the grip of one hand.

"I almost forgot," she said, holding the paper out to him. She watched him take it, his face a study in puzzlement. "Just fill in the amounts and give me the total. I'll write you a check."

He unfolded the slip and ran his eyes over her neatly compiled list. Without looking up, he inquired matter-of-factly, "What is this? Are you trying to make me lose my temper, Julia?"

"Of course not. It's just an accounting of what I owe you," she explained. Her eyes rounded as he refolded the paper, then deliberately ripped it in half, then half again. "What are you doing?" she demanded.

"We'll split the bills as they come, as we agreed, but what's already paid for is paid for. I don't want to hear any more about it."

"But—"

"You know, it's funny how faces can fool you," he interrupted. "I'd have said you were the last person on earth to be a troublemaker. You look so calm, not at all like someone who loves to argue."

He'd risen to stand before her, and Julie saw the teasing in his eyes, his curling lips, but she also saw a determination behind the amusement. She gave in gracefully.

"Then there's nothing left for me to say but thank you. And good night."

He stood motionless for several minutes after she left. He realized he'd been hoping she would defy him so he would have an excuse to touch her again, as he had in the kitchen. It slowly dawned on him that until he got her to bed, living with her was going to be an exquisite form of torture.

CHAPTER FOUR

Living with him was going to be an exquisite form of torture.

Julia realized this as she sidestepped a clutter of white jogging shoes and a scarlet sweat suit littering the kitchen floor. After a week she could almost pretend his constant siege on the neatness of their apartment no longer bothered her. No amount of imagination, however, could convince Julie that Cam himself didn't bother her. And in a much more elementally disconcerting way.

She went through the motions of preparing coffee, not watching what her hands were doing as images of Cam flashed through her mind. She pictured him dozing in rumpled ease on the study sofa, catching a stray kernel of popcorn on the tip of his tongue, backpedaling down the hallway to catch an imaginary touchdown pass. He often looked as if he found life amusing, as if he found *her* amusing. At other times his gaze traveled over her with a darkly disturbing intensity. He could be moody and dictatorial, seeming to resent the slightest disagreement to his casually tossed-out orders. He could be gentle and teasing, softening every command with a charm that took her breath away. She couldn't maintain her irritation with him and to be honest, she didn't even try.

Not even last night when he'd nearly blasted her out of the apartment with hours of ear-splitting rock 'n' roll. She endured as long as she could, then yielded the field, shutting herself in her room with cotton stuffed in her ears. Twenty minutes later a wary excitement lurched in her breast as her bedroom door opened.

"Room service," called Cam lightly as he entered. He carried a square wooden tray, which he set on her nightstand. Steam wafted lazily from the spout of a tall silver pot, four cookies formed a tiny pyramid on a plate, and a bag of miniature marshmallows leaned against a glazed pottery mug.

Julie watched, eyes wide and deep blue, as he sat on the edge of her bed and spoke. One of his imaginary footballs seemed to have lodged in her throat, obstructing her attempts to tell him she couldn't hear. She managed to shake her head mutely. He grinned in understanding. He leaned forward. Julie could feel the scratch of his charcoal wool sweater as his arm grazed her cheek. Her ears rang with the tingling of his touch as his fingers feathered the shell of her ears. He removed the bits of fluff. Beyond his quiet chuckling, it was mercifully silent.

"Room service," he repeated. "One soothing pot of hot cocoa to wash down a chocolate chip cookie for the mademoiselle." He poured cocoa into the mug and liberally dotted the surface with marshmallows. He then held the drink out to her.

Immobilized by the proximity of him on her bed, Julie could only sit and stare at the silvery halo the lamplight bestowed on his dark hair. He took her hand in his, then curled her fingers around the handle of the mug. Passing her the top cookie from the pyramid, he began munching on a second one. "Did you know," he asked conversationally, "that ninety-nine percent of the world's ills can be cured by chocolate chip cookies?"

Her breath sucked in on a laugh. A scalding gulp of hot cocoa eddied down her throat, and Julie choked. The mug was lifted from her hand, and she forgot the burning of her esophagus. Her attention was centered on the scorching of her shoulder where Cam's hand gently pounded. When she ceased coughing, she barked out a hoarse thank you, and he resumed eating another cookie.

"Tell me," he said after devouring it, "was my music too loud for you?"

She hesitated, then answered, "A little."

"Thank God for that," he said, and she sputtered. He bit into the last cookie. "I was afraid I was living with a woman who got her kicks by stuffing her ears full of cotton. Not that I'd object to a cotton fetish, mind you, but—"

Giggles bubbled within Julie. When she laughed outright, he pointed to her half-eaten cookie. "Are you going to eat that?" he asked, then snatched it from her before she could reply.

Despite layers of blankets, sheets, and flannel nightgown, Julie was conscious of his thigh pressing against her hip. She fought feeling the warmth of him and lost. Her entire body throbbed with an unsteady exhilaration. Sipping at her cocoa, she riveted her eyes on the lift beneath the covers where her knees were bent.

He rose, and her eyes raced to his. She felt bereft. But of course, she couldn't ask him to remain with her. So she licked melted marshmallow from her lips and murmured a paper-thin thank you.

Collecting the tray, Cam moved to the door. There he paused and half turned. "From now on, Julie, you must tell me when I disturb you," he told her firmly. "I'm not a mind reader."

She'd nodded, touched by his consideration. As the door clicked shut Julie had pulled in her lower lip and gnawed furiously. A new companionship seemed to have risen with the steam of the hot cocoa. She wasn't actually certain she wanted to overcome the slight constraint that had previously bound their relationship. She somehow felt safer for that bit of reserve between them. And yet . . .

Julia forced herself back to the sun-splashed reality of morning. She poured a cup of coffee then reached across the counter for the cream. Cameron was leaning against the frame of the door, watching her, his body oddly tense within the relaxed stance. A headless ghost couldn't have startled her more than his unexpectedly early appearance. Catching sight of him, Julie jumped, sloshing hot liquid onto the patterned linoleum.

He leaped forward at once. "Are you okay? Did you burn yourself again?" he asked, vainly attempting to take her hand in his.

"I'm fine, really. Not a drop on me," she said quickly. She pulled away and set the cup down on the counter behind her.

He wasn't wearing a shirt! She was amazed at the sudden acceleration of her heartbeat, the constriction of her throat at that brief glimpse of his muscular chest. She was also frightened. The way his body tapered from shoulder to hip, the hollow of his breastbone, the light dusting of dark hair over his tanned skin—she'd noticed all this within seconds, and it unnerved her that she had done so. His hair was damp, wisping at the ends, and the aroma of soap mingled with talc tantalized her. She realized he'd just come from a shower, and that unsettled her even more.

Trying not to take further note of him, she busied herself with opening the cupboard beneath the sink and pulling several sheets from a roll of paper towels. As she bent and wiped the spill from the floor, she added breathlessly, "I didn't expect to see you up so early."

"Totally uncivilized, I'll admit," he agreed. "I have a series of meetings this morning. But what about you? I thought you'd be lazing around in bed, enjoying the weekend. Or don't you believe in lazing around?"

"I work every other Saturday," Julie responded, ignoring his bantering. She refused to so much as glance in his direction, and yet, she was intensely aware of each of his movements. "And anyway I don't like sleeping in late. I feel as if I've missed the most vital time of the day."

"Ah, so you don't believe in lazing around," he said with a satisfied air. "I knew it. Too much of the American work ethic about you, Ms. Hollis."

She ignored this too. With her usual grace she straightened.

Cam stood before her. He took the soggy towels from her, briefly grazing her hand as he did so. Her nerves jangled with a sudden tingling message she didn't want to receive. While he deposited the towels in the trash, Julie leaned into the edge of the counter and attended to adding the cream to her coffee as if it were the prime reason for her existence on earth.

Though her hand was steady as he came to stand beside her, her heart was not. Her pulse marched through her veins in double time, and Julie didn't like the beat. Anxious to avoid even the merest contact with him, she hastily stepped away from the counter. She swallowed her urge to run from the room. She must not let him see what was happening to her.

Smoothing her brown-and-beige plaid skirt, she took one of the bright saffron chairs set before a small round table in the sunniest corner of the room. She could not, however, resist surreptitiously watching Cam. His jeans hung daringly low on his hips. She dropped her gaze. His feet were bare. Like his torso, she thought, and raised her eyes. He reached up to extract a mug from the cupboard, and the muscles in his smooth back stretched, then smoothed. Julie forced her eyes downward, focusing on the milky swirls in her coffee. She felt, rather than saw, Cam saunter toward her.

"Someone should have warned me that you were the original early bird," he said as he sat opposite her.

"Someone should have warned me about you," she retorted, then flushed as she remembered someone *had* and quite vociferously. She went on lightly, "You're the latest night owl I've met. And the latest riser. I didn't think you ever opened an eye before noon. It's little wonder you scared me so, appearing so unexpectedly just now."

"I defend myself on the grounds that any reasonable person would still be in bed at this ungodly hour of the day."

His prosaic tone steadied her. Julie realized she'd been behaving with the utmost foolishness, and slowly she began to relax.

She favored him with a half smile. "I suppose you mean to say that I'm unreasonable. I'm also a light sleeper."

"Did I bother you last night?" he asked with quick concern. As was his habit, after their tête-à-tête over cocoa and cookies he'd stayed up late into the early hours, encamped in the study.

Her smile widened. "No, not at all. I fail to understand, however, how you can listen to the stereo and watch TV at the same time."

"It's a gift," he said with a shrug. "Actually I don't pay much attention to either. They're just a background for my thoughts."

"I would think silence more conducive to thinking."

Though he drank his coffee black, Cam picked up Julie's spoon and clinked it around his mug several times. "Maybe for serious meditation," he said. "But I'm not given to that kind of thought. I asked you once if you meditate, do you remember?"

She did. She remembered everything about that first meeting. Before the Lambrusco anyway. However, she only nodded while sipping from her cup. She didn't want to encourage reminiscing, no matter how innocent it seemed.

"I tried to keep the stereo turned down," he said, suddenly sounding belligerent. She was looking more composed, less like the Julia he enjoyed seeing. He'd thought last night had been a breakthrough in their relationship, but gazing into her almost inanimate face, he realized he'd been indulging in wishful thinking.

"I know. I appreciate it," she responded. As he grew more restless she became calmer. His bared chest ceased to disturb her, and she scoffed inwardly at herself. Being so close to a half-dressed man—any man—was bound to elicit a strong reaction. After all, her natural responses had been repressed for far longer than many would consider healthy. Her rationalization cheered her; she smiled coolly at Cam, who dropped the spoon onto the table with a clatter.

"Sharing an apartment is possible only with compromise," he stated brusquely.

"Of course," she mildly agreed. "You know I'm willing to meet you halfway."

"Are you?"

Her smile vanished. There had been an uncalled-for intimation in his tone. "You know I am," she reaffirmed flatly.

He sipped his coffee and fiddled with her discarded spoon. He shot a piercing glance her way and suggested, "Then you might try loosening up a bit."

"Loosening up?" Her tone unconsciously dropped several degrees.

"That's what I'm talking about," he said, flipping the spoon away. With a quirk halfway between a smile and a frown, he said slowly, "You wouldn't melt in a frying pan on the hottest day in July. Whenever I come near you, you act about as thrilled as someone facing a doctor who's holding a foot-long hypodermic. If we're going to live together, Julia, we have to be on friendly terms. You have to quit being so uptight."

Her heart skittered erratically at the cajoling softness of his voice, at the velvet depth of his eyes. All her earlier confusion returned in a crashing floodtide. She wondered cynically just how friendly he wanted her to be and at the same time wondered what was wrong with her that she must question his motives. One certainty rose clear above the turmoil of her thoughts. She could not allow him to expect what she could not give.

Rising, she stated coolly, "This period of adjustment is rather awkward, but if we're both willing to give a little, we'll work it out. Now, I'm sorry, but I must leave. I have to open up the shop."

He didn't respond. She knew he was frowning heavily at her, but she couldn't take the time to soothe his ruffled feathers. She really did have to get to the bookstore. After rinsing her cup while Cam looked on in silence, she bade him good-bye and left. But Cameron continued to occupy her throughout the morning and well into the afternoon.

Was she so uptight? If so, it was mostly *his* fault, she decided irrationally. It was little wonder she was tense: she had not only to adjust to Cam, she had also to adjust to the extraordinary effect he had on her. Not that she wanted to adjust to it precisely. She wanted to make it go away.

Julie shook her head, clearing her mind of the unwanted thoughts of Cameron Stone. The list she'd been compiling swam into view, and she continued reading the last line she'd jotted on *A General History of... the Pirates:* "Spine rubbed, but otherwise a very good copy." She now added a price of forty dollars and moved to the next book to be entered into the summer catalog.

She neatly wrote down the next title then paused. Again she envisioned the corded sinews of Cam's bared arms, the crisping hairs curling against his chest. A muffled deprecatory laugh escaped her into the quiet solitude of the empty bookstore. Julie knew she was being foolish, but suddenly she didn't care. With an air of jubilant resolution she shoved her legal pad aside and cleared the countertop. She was going to close early.

It didn't take her long to balance the day's total and lock up the store. She didn't probe deeply into her motives. After all, it had been a slow day, with only a few customers trickling into the shop. Why shouldn't she go home early? It wasn't as if she were going home to be with Cam. He'd said he was going to several meetings. He might not even be home.

He was in the study, sprawling over the rust-colored sofa with an open leather briefcase at his feet and a can of beer at his hand. Papers were strewn carelessly around him. He seemed to be absorbed in watching the television and was unaware of her quiet entrance. Julie snatched at this opportunity to study him openly, lingering in the shadows just beyond the open doorway.

As she watched he swept his hand through his straight dark hair no less than three times, negligently tousling it. The long sleeves of his perse work shirt were casually rolled up on his forearms, the cuffs dangling in the air. One edge of the shirt was tucked into his faded jeans; the other hung out over the tooled leather belt.

An impulse to rearrange his shirt with her own hands streaked through her, shocking her. She pressed her hands together. Whatever was she thinking of? That was not the sort of relationship she wanted with this man!

He chuckled, and Julia turned her attention to the TV in the corner. Black-and-white images flickered over the screen. She recognized it as an old episode of *Leave It to Beaver.*

"Uplifting," she said dryly, stepping from the shadows and over the scattered sheets of paper.

Cam started, his gaze whisking from the screen to her face. He laughed as he straightened. "Don't be so disparaging. *Beaver*'s a slice of Americana."

Julia sat on the chair before the desk, her back as straight as the wood behind her. She crossed her feet demurely at the ankles and neatly smoothed her plaid wool skirt before looking at him. When she did, her brows were raised. "Oh, really?"

He frowned. God, how he hated her primness! With a nod to the TV he said crisply, "Watching a show like *Beaver* is a reminder of lost innocence. Families like that—if there ever were any like that—are certainly gone now."

"There are still families like that," she returned.

"Oh, really?" he mocked.

She watched as he began gathering his neglected papers into small piles. She waited until he had filled his briefcase and shut it with an efficient snap. Meeting his gaze directly, she said emphatically, "Really."

"Come on, Julie. This is the eighties. Do you seriously believe a woman exists who wears pearls and heels to vacuum her house?" He stabbed a finger toward Mrs. Cleaver on the screen.

"I wasn't talking about clothes. I was talking about the survival of the American family."

"And I'm telling you the American family à la the Cleavers simply doesn't exist."

He sounded so positive, so unalterably certain, that for a moment Julia couldn't think how to refute him. After a pause she stated quietly, "Where I come from, it does. People there still believe in the old ethics, in the importance of the family as a unit. In my hometown the family takes precedence over just about everything."

She could hear herself becoming insistent. She noted the glitter entering Cam's eyes, and fastened her own gaze on her hands lying folded on her lap, noting a smudge of ink on the sleeve of her sweater.

"Your hometown isn't exactly the center of modern life." He slid a sidelong glance over her as he took a sip of his beer. Leaning back into the sofa's corded cushions, he added, "Your problem is that you can't see beyond your middle-class midwestern mores. When are you going to wake up and realize just how outdated your ideas are?"

The warmth of the flush mounting her cheeks seemed to burn to her very soul. Allen had teased her about her old-fashioned notions too; he had poked fun at her straitlaced standards until she'd discarded them. A bitterness welled within her. *Look where his updated standards got me,* Julia thought.

"They may be outdated, but they're mine," she said a shade tartly. "I believe in what I say. I don't care what more 'modern' people want."

"You ought to reexamine your attitude, Julie. It's too restrictive."

The discussion was bringing up too many unwanted memories. How had they got into this anyway? Julie felt herself losing control. "Restrictive to whom?" she countered hotly.

Cameron felt a rush of desire as he beheld her face lighting up with vivid anger. "Us mostly. We could have some fun if you'd loosen up. Our arrangement could be a whole lot more interesting with a little spice added."

Julia sucked in her breath. *At last.* She'd been expecting a proposition of this nature for some time. Since he'd first seared her with one of his scorching looks, in fact. Her self-control rushed back with full force. She could deal with this. She chanced a glance over at him.

The look in his liquid brown eyes told her explicitly just what he'd meant by *fun.* After one brief encounter she turned away from the heated darkness of his gaze. She sat perfectly still, schooling her face into its tranquil mask.

"I think we've already had this discussion," she said blandly. "There's no sense in repeating it."

She stood, ready to leave the room, but Cam was in the threshold before her, blocking her way.

"Why don't you consider deepening our relationship?"

"The *depth* you're referring to, Cameron, goes about as deep as a thimble," she said, her voice brittle. "I'm not into superficial relationships."

"Neither am I. That's why I want you, Julie," he returned huskily.

Her heart distinctly flipped over. An unpleasant sensation flooded her, making her skin tingle. He stretched out a hand toward her. Julia stared at it in horror. She knew she could not let him touch her. She slipped back into the room and stood stiffly facing him from a safe distance.

"We could be good together," he coaxed on a susurration which at last stirred her into speech.

"I want something you can't provide," she snapped. "Responsibility and commitment. I'm looking for a husband, not a lover. Now, will you please excuse me?"

"No. Not until I've had my say. What you're looking for, Julie, is a dream that died with shows like *Leave It to Beaver.* What I'm offering is reality. With emotional commitment—"

"For as long as the good times last," she cut in fiercely.

"That's as long as any commitment lasts," he rejoined on a terse bite.

"Lifelong commitment is the only kind I'm interested in. For bad times as well as good. I've made it perfectly clear from the beginning that I won't settle for anything less. If you continue to badger me on this point, *roommate,* I'm afraid I shall have to move out."

His eyes narrowed. He studied her tension, and some of his own left him. His stance eased as he continued to eye her from across the room. At length he said simply, "You won't be moving out, Julia."

Before she could negate this statement of seeming fact, he pivoted and passed through the door opposite, into his room. Julie stared at the empty threshold and tried to regather her equilibrium.

One week. In just one week he had managed to undo all the discipline she'd exercised over her emotions in the last two years. No matter how she tried, she couldn't restrain her reactions to him. He annoyed her. He amused her. Most of all he attracted her.

There. It was out. She'd admitted it. But she would fight the force of his magnetism. It was too deadly to give in to. Cameron freely declared his stance against marriage—which was more than Allen had done, she reflected. At least Cam was honest. But she'd meant what she'd told him. She wanted a husband, stability, security. She had no intention of going through another brief, painful affair. Such a relationship not only went against her nature, it also promised another bruising of her heart. Julia wasn't about to let that happen again.

She would soon learn how wrong she could be.

Up at her usual early hour the next morning, she collected both a cup of coffee and the Sunday paper. She sat on the cobalt couch in the windowed niche off the living room. Morning sunshine splayed over her, trapping the gold in her hair and bathing her tight dove-gray turtleneck in a warm pool of light. Everything appeared brighter; last night's confrontation seemed light-years away. Julie now felt stronger and safer.

Having admitted that Cameron attracted her, Julie believed she could deal with it. She would remain friendly but reserved.

Or she would move out. She smiled, once again feeling sure of herself and began leisurely to peruse the section propped on her jean-clad knee.

It took her several seconds to realize the front door had opened. To her amazement Cam walked in. He glanced once in her direction, then ignored her as he hung his jacket in the closet. She saw that he wore the same perse shirt he'd had on the night before, only now with a greater amount of wrinkles. As he turned to proceed down the corridor she spoke up.

"Why on earth are you up so early? Where have you been?"

He took another step, then halted. His hand raked through his already rumpled hair, then Cam slowly faced her. A sheepish smile tilted the corners of his lips. "Mornin', Julie."

She didn't trouble herself to acknowledge his greeting. "Where have you gone out to this time of the morning?" she asked again.

"I haven't gone out," he corrected. He came toward her, watching how the morning sun streaked through her hair, enticing him to catch it. "Actually I've just come *in.*"

"*In?*" she parroted. She felt like someone who's walked into the middle of a movie and can't follow the action. "You've just come in?"

"I went out last night after you went to bed," he explained.

Studying his face, she noted that he hadn't yet shaved and that slight smudges darkened his eyes. The look in those brown eyes was intently searching and unaccountably accusatory. It was also unsettling. Julie couldn't hold his gaze.

Lowering her eyes to the print of the *Chicago Tribune,* she said nothing. The uneasiness that had followed yesterday's discussion sprang up anew between them. She thought of how Cam had gone back to work in his study while she'd taken up a book to read in the living room. For once Julie had been unable to lose herself in the magical world of a novel. She'd given up the attempt and gone to bed around ten. But she didn't remember hearing him leave.

"I didn't hear you go out," she said finally.

"I deliberately tried not to disturb you. As I meant to avoid doing this morning. I forgot how early you get up," he added on a cynical drawl.

Unwillingly her gaze returned to his face. He met it with a mocking smile. He looked more than simply tired. He looked dissatisfied, restless, almost unhappy, she thought. She wanted to know why.

"You went out last night, and you're just now coming in? What were you doing all night?"

As soon as the question popped from her lips Julie realized her naiveté. She fervently wished she could recall her words. She thought she would choke on her lack of sophistication. And it was all too clear that Cam both understood and enjoyed her discomfiture.

"Are you really so innocent?" he queried.

His tone told her just how amusing he found the situation. His attitude pricked her, and she snapped in shrill defense, "That's certainly more than can be said for *you*, isn't it? You're about as innocent as a rattlesnake! Tell me, will you be staying out all night often?"

Cam's amusement disappeared in a flash of annoyance. "I didn't expect to be grilled about my activities, least of all by you. You sound like a jealous fishwife—without, I might add, the least right to do so."

She bit her lip. She *had* sounded precisely like a jealous wife. It upset her as much as it did him. What did she care how Cam spent his nights?

"I'm sorry. You're right, of course." Snapping the newspaper to attention, Julia focused her unseeing gaze on the center of the page. She wished he would leave and let her recapture her pleasant morning.

It seemed she would get her wish. He made a move as if to leave, but after taking a step, he halted abruptly. "Julie, look at me," he ordered softly.

She stubbornly kept her eyes riveted on the engrossing fact that her local drugstore had laxatives on sale for half price. Other women might enjoy treating him as lord and master, but if he expected such blind obedience from *her,* Cameron Stone was due for a big disappointment.

"Julia."

Her name rustled on the air between them, uttered as gently as a spring breeze, yet carrying the sting of a whip. The crinkling of the newspaper as her hand tightened its grip was the only sound for several seconds. She heard him take a step toward her, and hastily she looked up at him.

It was too late. Cameron reached her in three sure strides. Grasping her arms in his hands, he hauled her to her feet. As the *Tribune* slipped unseen from her fingers, he pulled her against him. The beat of his heart thudded erratically against hers.

She gazed up into his glittering brown eyes from beneath half-dropped lids. A sense of inevitability took hold of her. It was as if the past two weeks had been building toward this moment and Julia no longer had the will to rebuff him. She stood motionless, scarcely daring to breathe, waiting.

It seemed an eternity before Cameron bent his lips to hers. He took her lips with a kiss of practiced persuasion, a kiss both determined and triumphant. She met his lips with a kiss of unwilling acceptance, a kiss passionate yet resistant.

He felt that resistance and it annoyed him. Cameron's kisses usually melted the women in his arms. Never had he wanted that effect more than now. Sliding his arms down to Julie's small, firm buttocks, he pressed her tightly against him.

The warmth of him, the hardened solidity of him, excited Julie beyond thinking of consequences. Her desire to withstand his assault ebbed on the rising tide of her physical need. Winding her arms about his neck, she played with the soft ends of his hair as they lay against his nape. Breathily she plumbed the pliant depths of his mouth with her tongue. She felt his body go taut.

Cam lifted his lips on a low moan. "Oh, Julie," he whispered. His breath swept lightly over her cheek. "Julie, I knew we'd be good together."

He knew as he spoke that he'd made a mistake. Julie stiffened within his hold, withdrawing from her impassioned response even as he sought to recapture her with another kiss. It did no good. His victory speech had been premature.

Cam's words had been like a cold dash of ice water over her heated senses. What for her was an awakening of volcanic force, was to him just another good-time episode. She knew his feelings had nothing to do with his physical desire; hers were inseparably entwined. She forced herself to think of Allen, and as she did, her ardor faded away. She remained listless within Cam's arms.

At length he realized he wasn't going to get anywhere and released her. She stood rigidly straight, head bent, hair falling like a gossamer veil over her flushed cheeks. He pivoted and strode away. At the door he paused, a half smile flitting across his lips.

"I wouldn't go out at all, Julia," he said huskily, "if you wanted to keep me here. Just remember that."

CHAPTER FIVE

Cameron's slight stock of patience was about depleted. He was unfamiliar with restraint, particularly where women were concerned, and the cool reserve of Miss Julia Hollis was beginning to exasperate him.

He tapped out an impatient beat upon the top of his desk and asked himself once again why he even cared. She was precisely the type of woman he most assiduously avoided—a woman with marriage on her mind. To top it off she had the personality of a limp noodle.

At that thought Cam sprang from his padded leather chair and paced the length of his plush office. He paused before the Plexiglas shelving filled with the utmost sophisticated stereo equipment and thought of Julie's musical laughter. He knew she wasn't as limp as she often pretended to be. He wished she were; then he wouldn't feel this overpowering need to discover every little thing about her.

Flinging himself onto one of the deep purple chairs facing the glass wall, he clamped a set of headphones on and flicked a button that was set into the arm. He didn't listen to the music and he didn't look at the view of the Marina Towers beyond the plate-glass window. He occupied himself, as he had all morning, with thoughts of Julia.

She could be so still, her placidity irritating him to the point of madness. Then, unexpectedly, she would come vividly to life, her face filling with rare animation. She reminded him then of a flower gracefully unfolding its petals to emit a heady fragrance. She had a knack of listening to him with an exceptional attentiveness, her entire being seeming to be concentrated on him. At such times she appeared approachable, but whenever he reached for her, Julie would withdraw with the elusiveness of a butterfly.

The conflict of their schedules had kept them apart more than together over the past week. Yet Cam was acutely aware of Julia's presence. He'd come into the kitchen for breakfast, and the lingering scent of her perfume would tease him, reminding him she'd just left. The morning newspaper would be neatly folded and awaiting him on the small breakfast table. Her cup would be rinsed and draining on the countertop. Each day was filled with such tantalizing hints of her existence. Each day Cam would look forward to the brief time they would share.

But when they were together, Julie maintained a reserve toward him that would have left ice on the equator. He knew he'd made a mistake in suggesting they become lovers. He hadn't meant to speak up so soon. But when she'd begun arguing with him, she'd flashed fervently to life. He envisioned her sitting so primly, lips ardently parted as she stressed her point. Her thin, translucent face had colored with a kissable beauty. Her blue eyes had sparked flames that ignited his need.

He wanted her.

He shifted in the chair. He hadn't even realized how much he wanted Julie until he'd gone out Saturday night. He'd been intent on releasing his pent-up frustrations with a vivacious friend he knew he could rely on for a good time. Yet, he'd stayed at her apartment for less than twenty minutes, eager to leave the minute he arrived. He'd ended up drinking at bars and driving around until dawn.

Julie's apparent jealousy had elated him, and he'd stoked it higher with innuendos that had no foundation in fact. Now he wondered if what he'd thought was jealousy had in reality been mere prudishness. He recalled their argument that morning. He felt again the softness of her beneath his hands. He could almost taste again the breathy warmth of her kiss. . . .

The memory stirred him. He pulled off the headphones and tossed them onto the empty chair beside him. With unwarranted force he switched off the spinning reel-to-reel tape, then slammed purposefully out of his office, barely pausing to inform his secretary he was leaving.

He wanted her and he meant to have her.

"What is all this?" queried Julia in the tone one might use upon catching someone in the cookie jar red-handed.

She eyed the softly glowing candles that surrounded a single rose in a long-necked vase and the fire flickering in the grate with equal wariness. A linen tablecloth was spread out in front of the fire with two glasses and an icebucket positioned on one corner. A bottle of champagne, tilted within its bed of ice, was a clear signal of Cam's intentions. Completing her visual tour of this calculated setting for romance, her gaze settled on Cameron.

"Are you expecting someone?" she inquired coldly.

He met her condemning eyes with choirboy innocence. "Don't be looking down that classic nose of yours. I thought you might want to relax after such a long day at work."

Relax? she thought cynically. She was certain that wasn't what he meant in the least. Determined though she was not to be affected by that charming tilt of his lips or velvety tone of his voice, Julie's heart was leaping convulsively. She began to move away from him, toward the refuge of her own room.

"Thanks," she said in that same chilled voice, "but I intend to do just that by going straight to bed. Good night."

He shadowed her down the long corridor until at last Julie halted and turned. "What are you doing?" she demanded.

"I'm going to run some bathwater for you," he replied blandly.

"What!"

"You're as wound up as an eight-day clock. What you need

is a long soak in a hot tub." He wheeled her around and nudged her onward. "I hereby swear I'm not intending to leap into the water with you. Just get your things together, and I'll take care of your bath."

She dug in her heels and turned, ready to argue. He set two fingers on her lips, stilling her protest. "Julia, you've just put in a twelve-hour day. You need to relax before you try to sleep or you'll be too keyed up to rest. You may think you're so tired you'll fall asleep immediately, but I'm willing to bet once you lie down, you'll start tossing and turning."

He gave her no time to argue this logic, but propelled her into her bedroom, where she stood wavering. Even if what he did say made sense, it didn't explain the carefully seductive setup in the living room. She heard the water running in the bathroom and knew Cam would be perfectly capable of throwing her into the tub if she didn't go willingly. Sighing, she began to gather together her underwear, white flannel nightgown, and furry robe.

Let him try seducing me in these, she thought with a faint return to humor.

Kicking off her shoes, Julie suddenly realized just how weary she felt. A shipment of books purchased from an estate sale had arrived that morning, and she'd stayed on into the night to look them over, separating them into groups to begin the process of evaluating and pricing. Once begun, she'd become, as always, enthralled with her work. She suspected she'd still be at the shop, immersed in dusty books with such intriguing titles as *Wimples and Curling Pins* or *Stand and Deliver: The Story of the Highwaymen,* if Cameron had not called there shortly after ten demanding to know what the hell she was doing.

Only with a great deal of fast talking and promising to come home immediately had she been able to convince Cam not to come after her. And then she'd walked into that so well thought out romantic scene. Her first reaction had been anger mingled with panic. Anger at his obvious attempt to change their relationship; panic because she feared he would succeed.

Ever since Cam had held her in his arms the week before, Julie had been caught in a turmoil of feelings. She worried he would touch her again; she felt disappointed when he did not. She was relieved when he left her alone and depressed when he didn't make time to be with her. At night she would touch a finger to her lips, imagining the feel of his once again, then angrily tell herself to stop being foolish.

Her thoughts infuriated her, yet Julie felt powerless to stop them. The constant battle of her emotions left her feeling confused, but she was certain of one thing. She must not allow Cameron to make love to her. She couldn't bear the pain of being one of his playthings.

Whatever he had in mind for tonight wouldn't include her, she determined with a forceful shake of her head. She would simply dart from her bath to her bed before he had the opportunity to make use of the champagne and candles.

She removed her stockings and neatly folded them into her drawer, then swept her hair upward and skewered it carelessly into place. Glancing into the dresser mirror to check the effect, Julia caught sight of the rose standing on the nightstand beside her bed. As if hoping it were a mirage, she shut her eyes and slowly turned.

She opened her eyes. The rose leaned gently toward her pillow, its petals unfurled.

Damn him, she thought furiously. She wasn't about to fall for such tricks twice and the sooner she made this clear to him, the better. She snatched up a pair of hangers for her blouse and skirt and marched out with her head defiantly high.

He was waiting by the door of the bathroom, leaning against the frame with a lingering smile upon his lips. "I was just about to come and get you," he said, softly teasing.

She ignored this. "Excuse me," she said in a tight voice as she attempted to push past him.

Though barely moving, Cameron managed to check her movement. He ran a finger lightly down her nose, infuriating her.

If her arms hadn't been filled with clothes and hangers, Julia would have slapped the assured smile off his sensual lips. As it was, she stood silently seething.

"Relax, little one," he murmured. He traced the curve of her lips with his finger, then straightened. "Enjoy your bath," he said as he sauntered away.

She flung open the door and paused on the threshold, stunned. Candlelight danced over capricious shadows, and an aroma of strawberries drifted over her. Julie narrowed her eyes at the provocative incandescence radiating from the branched candelabrum, a silver antique Grams had given her, then widened them at the mysterious bag tied with bright red ribbons that was dangling from the faucet. On the tray spanning the width of the tub stood yet another red rose in a crystal vase and beside it a single glass of champagne.

My, my, my, she said to herself as she finally moved into the room and shut the door, *what have we here?* She slipped out of her clothes, hanging them up with hands that shook slightly. Julia was, at heart, a romantic. She stood naked in the luminescent candlelight and strove not to be overcome by Cam's romantic efforts. Cynicism was what she needed now, and Julie summoned up a heavy dose of it.

When she slipped into the warm water, the strawberry scent enveloped her. Fizzing bubbles surrounded her, and she felt the slick sheen of oil caressing her skin. She held up the glass in a silent toast. You had to hand it to the man. He certainly knew how to steal your breath away. Not even Allen had ever thought of presenting her with a strawberry-champagne bath.

Stretching languorously, Julie watched the hypnotic waverings of the candleflames. The tension of the day seeped out into the scented water. She lay content, occasionally sipping champagne and lazily splashing water. This was, she decided, the perfect way to end a workday.

A tapping at the door disturbed her. She opened an eye,

realized she been dozing, and yawned. "Yes?" she mumbled through her yawn.

"Unless you want to be known as this year's Miss Prune, you'd better get out now, Julie," said Cam in a voice that reached through the door to stroke her tenderly.

She merely purred in response. Cameron waited several seconds, then rattled the doorknob. "Julia, don't fall asleep in there. If you do, I'll have to come in and get you."

That woke her up. She knew he would, locked door or no. "All right, Cam," she called out. She sat up, making deliberate noise as she did so. She listened for his retreat, cursing her pounding heart for deafening her. When she at last heard his receding footsteps, she rose from the tub.

She leisurely toweled herself dry, then dusted herself with talc. Donning her voluminous nightgown, she smiled at her steam-rouged reflection and brushed her teeth. She threw on her robe and blew out the candles. Collecting her clothes, she quietly unlocked the door. She would slip into the safety of her room and politely thank Cam in the morning for the trouble he'd taken with her bath.

She walked directly into a wall of firmly muscled chest. The haphazard pile of hair atop her head threatened to topple as she threw back her head to glare at Cam.

A wicked smile danced over his lips. "Let me help you," he said on a light laugh. With a gallant flourish, he removed the bundle in her arms.

"That's quite all right," returned Julia through tight lips. She made an attempt to retrieve her clothes. He held them away from her with infuriating ease, then pressed her toward the living room.

"Did you enjoy your bath?" he asked softly.

"Yes," she barked, sounding rather as though she'd hated it. "I wish to go to bed now, if you please," she added stiffly.

"I don't please," he immediately retorted. He again pushed

her gently away from her bedroom. "Now, be a good girl and let me get this cleaned up."

She saw that beneath his laughter ran an iron bar of unyielding determination. With a disdainful huff, she whirled and swept grandly down the hall. He obviously meant to seduce her tonight.

Her senses leaped at the thought.

She snubbed the linen cloth spread so invitingly before the fire and placed herself rigidly upon one of the flowered wingback chairs. She felt ridiculous, out of place in this romantic setting with her loosely clamped twist of hair, her furry robe and flannel nightie, her bare feet. She didn't belong. Surely Cameron would see that too.

He paused just beyond the living room, staring at Julia. She looked like a child, her figure hidden by the ugliest furred chartreuse robe he'd ever seen. Candlelight laced gold ribbons through the knot of hair sitting crookedly atop her head. Her back was stiff, and her lips were pressed into a thin line of disapproval. She was the farthest thing from a femme fatale he could imagine, yet Cam had never experienced such a rush of overwhelming hunger for a woman.

"Champagne, little one?" he asked as he drew into the room.

"No, thank you," she replied with cutting accents.

He smiled widely, amused at her virtuous attitude. Tonight, he thought, whatever she did would amuse him. He strolled to the bucket and unconcernedly uncorked the bottle. Its resounding pop cracked through the silence blanketing them. He poured a glass, then another. Julie watched this with hostile eyes that flashed daggers as he brought one to her.

"I told you—"

"No one likes to drink champagne alone," he told her reproachfully.

He unnerved her by dropping onto the arm of her chair. His thigh brushed against her arm, and for an instant Julie couldn't breathe. She inched into the opposite corner, wishing the chair were wider.

"Now," he said in a casually conversational tone, "what shall we talk about? Should we discuss your work today or mine? Or perhaps your childhood? How about your first love?"

She gasped and threw him a wide-eyed look of shock. This wasn't what she'd been expecting! She'd thought he'd tell her how her lips were like rubies or her eyes like stars or some other such meaningless flattery. Then she could have reacted with the cool passivity she knew he so disliked. As it was, caught off-guard, Julia immediately flushed. She turned her head, focusing on the splashes of white and pink against the blue arm of the chair.

So there had been a first love. Cam didn't know whether he was relieved or oddly annoyed. He gazed at the candlelit curve of her cheek, the golden tendril slipping over her ear. "Would you like to hear about my first love?" he queried lightly.

"You can remember that far back?" she returned on a flare of animosity. She was flustered and she didn't like it. Why did he have the ability to disconcert her so?

He chuckled softly. "Just barely. I was ten; she was twelve. She had flaming red hair and could climb a tree faster and throw a softball harder than any boy. I thought she was magnificent."

Despite herself Julie smiled at the image of Cam at ten, mooning over a carrot-topped tomboy. Forgetting her resolve not to, she sipped her champagne. "So what happened?" she asked.

"I tried to impress her by showing her how tough I was. I fell from the top bar of the jungle gym at school and broke my arm. End of romance," he said with a grin.

Julia laughed.

She outsparkles champagne, he thought, and had to restrain himself from voicing it. Instead, he continued in the same friendly tones, "Your turn. Who did you love at ten?"

"No one. That is, no one real. I read *Little Men* nine times that summer and *Eight Cousins* twice. No boys I knew could match the ones I read about." Julie looked into the bubbling amber and said wistfully, "I've never related easily to people, not even as a child. Grams always said my well ran deep, but once tapped—" She broke off as she realized what she was confiding. To cover her confusion she quickly gulped the rest of her drink.

Cam took the empty glass and refilled it. He sat down by the ice bucket and patted the spot beside him. "Come sit over here, Julie."

She hesitated, but he was looking at her in a manner more amicable than ardent, so she joined him on the cloth, sitting Indian-style while facing the lazily wavering fire. Cameron rose in one lithe motion and began to stoke the flames into a leaping roar of life. She inspected him covertly, admiring the shape of his body. He wore a mauve crew-neck sweater and snug-fitting jeans. He looked comfortably casual. And to her, dangerously desirable.

He slid into place next to her—so close, she could feel the heat radiate from his body, the flexing of his muscles as he brought his glass to his lips. "Sooo," he drawled, "If you won't tell me about your first love . . ." He waited, and Julie held her breath. "Tell me about your dreams instead."

"Dreams?" she squeaked.

He leaned toward her and took her glass from her hands. He chased the amber bubbles of champagne with his fingertip. "You know, dreams. Visions. Aspirations." He paused, then lowered his voice to a husky rasp. "Desires."

Julia stared at the fizz clinging to his finger. Mesmerized, her gaze followed the path of his finger as he slowly drew it from the champagne, slowly brought it to her lips, slowly set it against the sensitized tip of her tongue.

"You have them, don't you?" he prodded in a rustling voice.

The flavor of his skin rippled along her taste buds. She couldn't pull her eyes away from the molten intensity of his.

"Don't you?" he asked again.

"Ummm," she agreed, her upper lip humming against his trimmed nail.

"So tell me," urged Cam. He withdrew his finger and handed her the glass.

"Oh, dear, well . . ." said Julia, stalling. She sipped the champagne and strove to summon up an answer that wouldn't reveal any of her true desires. "Like the seasons, dreams change. When I was young—"

"Younger."

"A mere babe," she amended. "Anyway I wanted to be a horse." Cam choked on a mixture of laughter and amber liquid and she expanded on a whimsical note, "When I found out I could never, ever be a horse, I settled for becoming a manager of a secondhand bookshop."

"And now?"

"Well, now, I rather think my ambition is to have my glass refilled."

He obliged with a laugh and gracefully gave up his attempt to probe. Instead, he turned the conversation to a lighthearted accounting of his search for a certain obscure brand of homemade noodles. The rock group Whiplash would be coming into town for a concert later this summer, he told her, and the lead singer, Mike Rivers, had stipulated in the contract that he be fed this particular brand of noodles.

"Is *that* what you do for a living?" she asked in disbelief, then listened in high enjoyment as he entertained her with similar anecdotes relating the headaches of pampering today's stars. Occasionally they lapsed into companionable silence, content to simply sit together in the firelight. Gradually they emptied the bottle. Julie wasn't quite certain just when Cameron had replaced it, but she realized she'd made quite a dent in the second bottle when she found him leaning over her, slipping her robe off her shoulders.

"Cam, please," she protested feebly then.

"Julia, please," he mocked on a silken whisper. Then he stated firmly, "You're too warm, you're perspiring—"

"I'll move back, away from the fire," she interrupted quickly as he shook her arm free of one sleeve.

"Don't be such a prude," he murmured.

"I'm not! It's just, it's just—"

"It's just that you're a little prude," he finished with a low laugh. He tossed her robe beyond her reach, then laughed more fully as he caught sight of her nightgown. "God. Do you wear a chastity belt underneath that thing as well?"

"Don't be snide," sniffed Julie tilting her nose into the air. "This is a very respectable article of night apparel," she explained, carefully enunciating each word.

"That's the problem," he drawled provocatively.

"What is?" she asked with a puzzled frown.

"It's too damned respectable," he replied like a cat pouncing on its prey.

Self-consciously, she stared down into the folds of flannel. It more than adequately covered her. She told herself not to worry about the robe. She *had* been too warm, after all. And as he said, the gown was perfectly respectable. She raised her eyes and was directly hit with the full force of Cam's darkly disturbing gaze. He no longer appeared amicable in the least.

Bewildered, she again inspected her gown. What had put that hot blaze of desire into his eyes? She shook her head and decided to ask him. Her mouth opened, but only a tiny squawk came out as she felt herself pressed back to the floor. The weight of Cameron's body settled gently against her, and Julia's bewilderment gave way to alarm.

"What are you doing?" she demanded in a voice meant to be daunting. It wasn't.

"This," whispered Cam, placing his lips into the curve of her long neck.

Her pulse careened wildly beneath his lips. Julia trembled as his tantalizing tongue flicked against her skin. She tried to tamp her rising excitement, but the exquisite pleasure of his touch defeated her. She felt her resistance melting away with each long smooth stroke of his hands over her arms.

This man knows what he's doing flashed through Julia's mind, but even that cynical thought didn't stop her from responding to his well-placed kisses and his calculated caresses.

Very gently Cam slid his hands over her shoulders and to the short row of buttons fastening the neck of her nightgown. As he undid them his lips traced the hollow of her throat, the rise of her collarbone. He tasted the strawberry fragrance of her skin. He heard the quickening of her breath and felt the warmth of it stir against his hair.

Cameron's hands dropped lower to circle the swell of her hips, evasive in the fluffy folds of her gown. He wanted to tell her how soft she was, how beautiful, but he wasn't going to repeat his previous mistake. He had better uses for his lips. He nuzzled the smooth contour of her breast with his mouth, lightly kissing and teasing with his tongue.

Julie heard a low sigh, nearly a moan, and was surprised to recognize that it came from her lips. The urgent need to touch him, to thread her fingers in his hair, to run her hands down the supple muscles of his back, overwhelmed her. She tried to pull her hands from beneath Cam's imprisoning hold.

He misunderstood her action and let his weight fall heavily against her, constricting her movement. Cradling her head between his palms, he nibbled at her lips, once, twice. Then with an intense thrusting, he kissed her with all the pent-up passion he'd endured the last few weeks.

She met his kiss with a fierce delight that shocked them both. She arched toward him, throbbing with desire. She wrenched her hands free and pressed her fingers into his back, kneading the sinews beneath the wool of his sweater. She wanted to know the feel of him, the taste of him, the pleasure of him.

They swayed together in a spiral of passion. They kissed and nibbled and touched with feverish haste. Electric sensations raced from one to the other as each kiss went deeper and deeper, generating an excitement far beyond any either had ever known.

Cameron drew back, slightly dazed at Julie's ardent response. He stared at the firelit planes of her face. Gone was the nunlike repose he so disliked. Beneath her droopy lids, her eyes were darkly dilated with passion. Her usually pale cheeks were colored with a heated rose; her lips were full and begging to be kissed. Her hair had tumbled free of its clasp and cascaded in captivating disarray about her face. In the gleam of the fire it sparkled like an amber halo. It was the way he'd most yearned to see her. And yet . . .

"Julia?" he said, his voice questioning.

She mewed softly. She thrust her hands into his hair, trying to force his lips back to hers. Cam thwarted her by pulling farther away. An unexpected and unwanted conscience shrouded his excitement. How much of this pulsating need of hers was due to him and how much to the champagne? Would she give in to him now but hate him in the morning? And did it matter?

With a silent groan Cameron admitted that it did. He now realized he wanted her to come to him of her own sober will. He didn't want her to repudiate making love to him—not because of candlelight, not because of champagne, not because of anything. He tensed as Julie slid her hand beneath his sweater to rub along the flat planes of his stomach. Her touch felt cool against his heated skin. He sucked in a harsh breath and roughly shoved her hand away.

"Julie, for God's sake, don't!" he hissed.

"Why not?" she queried breathlessly.

He shot a sharp glare at her. Her lashes were dusting her cheeks and her lips were parted invitingly. He looked away. "Because if we don't stop now, we won't stop, period."

She frowned. The tip of her tongue poked out over her lip as she considered this. "Oh," she said in a high voice that confirmed Cam's worst suspicion.

Glancing at her, he saw her bat her eyelashes in an inexpert attempt to be coquettish. "Why should we stop?" she inquired.

He leaned over her and brushed her lips briefly with his. Drawing back, he said thickly, "Because you don't know what you're doing, and—"

"Yes, I do!" she objected instantly, highly offended.

"Then tell me, what are you doing?" He was half amused, half angry with her. She was so damn desirable, but he couldn't take advantage of her like this.

"I'm—I'm—" she stammered. A deeper layer of color mounted her cheeks. Abruptly, Julie sat up.

What *was* she doing? She glanced at Cam's mussed hair and rumpled sweater, then at her own dishevelment. It was all too apparent what she'd been doing. In that instant the champagne-induced haze cleared, and Julie realized how close she'd come to giving herself completely to Cam. She felt his eyes boring through her and bent her head, biting her lip.

"Exactly," said Cam tersely. "You'd better get to bed now, Julia. Alone."

She scrambled to her feet in instant obedience. Sweeping up her robe, she clutched its furry cloth to her breast and darted toward the hall. At the entrance, however, she paused, then slowly turned.

"Why did you stop, Cam?" she asked on a thread of a whisper.

He sat staring into the dying fire. After a stretch of silence he said without looking at her, "I don't know. Now, go to bed, Julia. Before I change my mind."

In a swirl of white flannel she whisked down the hall before he could. She experienced a wave of thankfulness for his surprising chivalry. It was immediately followed by an equal crest of regret.

CHAPTER SIX

Sunlight linked gilt chains across the pillow. Julia opened an eye into the light, groaned, and shut it again. For a woman who'd never had a hangover before a few weeks ago, she felt herself rapidly becoming a candidate for Alcoholics Anonymous.

Her head was thumping. She burrowed further into her pillow. Maybe if she lay very still, the sun would go away. She prayed for the rattling in her head to cease and vowed never to drink anything stronger than iced tea again. Gradually she realized the odd clinking she heard was *not* coming from her head. She slowly peeked through her lashes and promptly bolted upright.

"Mornin', Goldilocks," said Cam cheerfully as he whisked a spoon round a tall glass. "Headache?"

She glowered meaningfully at him and pressed her palms against her temples. It was not only her head that continued to throb painfully; her stomach was whirling, and her heart was doing odd little flip-flops. How long had he been standing beside her bed? It disturbed her to think of him watching her when she was unaware, when she was vulnerable.

And how, she instantly wondered, could he be looking so damn friendly? He should be overwhelmed with guilt! Why was she feeling so awkward and tongue-tied? *He* was the one who should be chagrined!

Her thoughts passed over her face like a weather bulletin over a TV screen. Cameron grinned and thrust the glass into her hand. "Drink this. It'll make you feel better."

Julie sniffed at it suspiciously. Something acrid tartly tingled her nostrils. Darting a glance at him, she inquired through the cotton in her mouth, "What is it?"

"Just drink up," he ordered.

She really was in no condition to argue. Even if it were poison, at least it would put her out of her misery. She tipped the cool glass against her lips and drank. Almost immediately she pulled it away. The concoction was both sour and spicy.

"What—" she began, but Cam effectively stopped her question by forcibly pressing the glass back to her lips. Cold liquid filled her mouth and dribbled down her chin. She had no choice but to swallow. He held it there until she'd downed nearly all of the noxious-tasting liquid.

Coughing and sputtering, Julie hotly demanded to know if he was trying to kill her.

Her anger was drowned in a wave of alarm as he settled himself on the edge of the bed beside her. As he began calmly wiping her chin off with the hem of the sheet, Julie stared into the seemingly endless depths of his dark eyes and felt all her desire of the previous night flare to renewed life.

Afraid he would read her feelings in her eyes, Julie dropped her lashes. She felt the heat of his touch through the flowered percale. He leaned toward her, and her heart pounded furiously. It was a wonder he didn't hear it. When his hand at last left her chin, she almost sighed audibly in relief.

"Do you feel better?" he asked.

"Yes. Yes, I do," she answered, and was surprised at the truth of it.

She chanced a quick look at him. He sat quarter-turned toward her, one leg drawn up on the bed, the other dangling over the edge. He wore a long-sleeved cranberry shirt, tan cord slacks, and a smile that left her weaker than a case of champagne.

"W-what was that vile stuff?" she inquired in an attempt to distract herself from his presence.

"Lime juice with a dash of Tabasco and crushed red peppers."

He laughed lightly at her immediate moue of distaste. "Settles the stomach and clears the head. Two aspirins and Doc Stone will have you on your way."

Her grimace faded to a slow smile. The sun sat fully upon her now, touching her hair with an aureole that took Cam's breath away. He stretched out a hand and gently laid a fingertip against her cheek.

"Are you willing this morning to finish what we began last night?" he quietly asked.

Her skin burned where his fingertip softly stroked and her nerves danced out of control. Her breath lodged in her throat and her heart knocked against her ribs. She couldn't speak.

"Are you?" he repeated, his voice harshly insistent.

Her heart said one thing and her mind said another. She had to try three times before her croaked whisper got out. "No."

A rueful smile twisted his lips. "I thought not. That's why I put a stop to it, Julie. I'm sorry about last night. It was a cheap shot."

She licked her dry lips. "I—that's okay. I understand."

"Do you?"

His finger trailed the line of her jaw and down her throat, pausing at the hollow. Leisurely Cam brought the whole of his hand to caress her neck. Her pulse fluttered against his palm. As his fingers delicately teased their way lower, a bursting sensitivity surged through Julie.

She was suddenly vividly aware of the warm caress of the morning sun and the heavy scent of the rose tilting in its vase. She heard the intake and release of their mingling breaths and the creak of the bed as Cam shifted closer. She felt the pressure of his thigh as it rested against hers and the stir of his arm as it reached toward her. Above all, Julie was heart-stoppingly aware of the tremor of her nerves in response to Cam's lingering touch.

She remembered she'd never rebuttoned her gown. It wasn't exactly a plunging décolletage, but it opened low enough to expose the topswell of her breasts. She knew he'd already discovered this; discovered it last night with his nuzzling lips. Panicking at the memory, she knocked his hand away.

Cameron studied her for what seemed a timeless moment. He lowered his lashes over his eyes, and she was amazed anew at how long and thick they were. Then he lifted them, and she was stunned at the passion blazing in his eyes.

"I still want you, Julia," he told her in a voice which breathed his desire.

Julie felt so dizzy, she was surprised when she didn't faint. Flustered, she looked beyond Cam's shoulder into the mirror over her dresser. She saw herself, sleep-tousled and excessively pale. She stared into her widened eyes and she saw the truth.

By far too honest to lie to herself Julie admitted that she wanted Cam too. It hadn't just been the champagne last night. She'd allowed herself to feel freer, more willing, because she'd known she could blame it on the alcohol. In the clear light of day, however, she had no one to blame but herself for feeling such an overwhelming hunger for him.

She couldn't hide it from herself, but she would have to hide it from him. If she allowed the least hint of her desires to show, the result would be bitterly painful. She knew what she wanted out of a relationship, and she knew Cam wasn't willing to provide it. To acknowledge her feelings for him she would have to accept him on his terms—terms that would crush her when they eventually parted.

Bringing her eyes back to his face, she said with amazing control, "You may want, but you can't have."

Tender humor radiated in his gaze. "Maybe not. But I'm damn well going to try."

Julie's only reply was a raised brow. But her heart skittered wildly at the deepening warmth within his appraisal of her.

"I'm too old to run after a woman I want," he said directly. "I'd far rather we came together naturally. But I want you, Julia, in a way I haven't wanted a woman before. If I have to, I'll stalk you with whatever weapon it takes."

"The big game hunter," she said in a voice nearly as dry as her mouth.

"That's right." He tapped the tip of her nose with his finger. "And be warned—it's open season on Julie."

He stood before she could think to react to his cocksure attitude. She was spinning like a carousel from his abrupt assault of her innermost desires. Hands on his hips, he grinned and asked what she would like to do with the day.

"Do?"

"March is too cold for a Sunday picnic, and it's too sunny to be shut inside a dark theater. How about the museum?"

She stared at him as if he had spoken in a foreign tongue. "What?"

"Think about the Art Institute while you get dressed. I'll get breakfast together," he tossed out as he headed for the door. There he paused. "And darling?"

"Yes?" she responded, before realizing the endearment.

"Brush your teeth thoroughly. Your breath is less than enchanting this morning."

She flung her pillow at a door already closing.

Though her head was still aching, she rose with amazing energy. He may be more dangerous than a nuclear warhead, but hadn't someone once said danger was stimulating? She'd told Mary Beth she wanted a change, and she couldn't deny she'd got it. She felt more alive this moment—massive headache and all—than she'd felt in two years.

Within minutes she was dressed in a pair of camel wool slacks and a bone-white Oxford cloth shirt. She'd downed two aspirins and combed her hair neatly into place. Her bed was made and her teeth were brushed—thoroughly.

As she joined Cam in the dining room he raised his head from the comics to flash her an approving smile. "You look better. How do you feel? Still grouchy?"

"I wasn't—"

"Sexual frustration will do that to a person, you know," he interrupted airily.

"I wasn't grouchy!" she finished with a snap.

"Ladies in good humor do not throw pillows at gentlemen," he chided in smug tones.

"Neither," returned Julia sweetly, "do I."

He laughed and leaned forward to proffer a plate of toast. She eyed it with extreme distaste. "No, thank you, I couldn't—"

"You should eat. It will help stave off the queasy feeling."

"More of Doc Stone's advice?" she asked tartly.

"Darn right. And darn good advice too." He waved the plate under her nose, and with a sigh Julie gave in and took a slice.

For a time she sipped orange juice and ate while Cam read the sports section. He reached blindly for his cup just as she reached for the jar of juice, and their hands bumped together. Their eyes instantly locked. She drew back as if struck. He let his hand linger in the air, then slowly took up his coffee cup. He watched her as he sipped and she could feel herself going red.

She recognized the excitement that flashed through his eyes and strove to calm herself. She picked up her toast. He continued to stare at her. Julie dropped the toast and glared at him.

"We have a perfectly fine living arrangement. Why are you so set on ruining it?"

"I happen to think making love to you would be an improvement on our relationship," he began.

She cut him off briskly. "I'm incapable of indulging in a light affair, Cam. The sooner you realize this, the better for both of us."

"Who said anything about keeping it light?"

The teasing tone stung Julia. To him this was apparently a big joke. His conquest of her had nothing to do with *her*. It was a sop to his masculinity, a proof that no woman could resist his overpowering charms. The thought should have angered her; it depressed her instead.

"I could just move out," she said in a shaken voice.

"You could," he agreed. "It wouldn't matter, Julie. I'll follow you if you leave. You've gotten under my skin and I want to get under yours."

"It's not that simple!" she burst out.

Instantly she subsided into her chair. This wasn't going as she'd hoped it would. How long could she resist her own desires in the face of his determination?

He watched the blue of her eyes fade to a sad gray and the width of her lips turn in a melancholy frown. It made her face seem longer, narrower, less appealing. He felt a renewal of that odd resentment of her that so often pricked at him. In the same heartbeat he longed to kiss away her sadness. He couldn't understand it any more than she could.

"You're right," he said tonelessly as he pushed back his chair. "It's not simple at all. But for now let's say we forget about everything except the Art Institute. It opens at one, and it's just about noon now, so—"

"It's that late?" She sounded shocked. She was. She only slept that late when she was seriously ill.

"It is," he replied firmly. "I think you'd have slept until dawn tomorrow if I hadn't drawn your curtains and rousted you from your beauty sleep."

She good-naturedly disputed this as they cleared the dishes and prepared to leave. But a guarded silence settled over them as they drove off in Cam's sleek silver Jag. Buds struggled to burst from branches in the brilliantly warm sunshine. Julie tried to concentrate on the beauty of spring, but her peripheral vision was dominated by the movement of tan corduroy tightly stretched over the muscles of Cam's thigh. Each time his cranberry sleeve lifted to shift gears, her heartbeat shifted speed. She propped her head against the leather headrest and closed her eyes.

While Cam's pronouncement of his intentions had both angered and agitated Julie, it had also secretly thrilled her. It was flattering to be wanted by a man like Cameron Stone. It was also dangerous. She had not the least intention of letting him succeed, and yet her traitorous mind wondered if he would. She catalogued the painful consequences of giving in to a charming playboy. And she recalled the pleasurable intoxication of the touch and taste and feel of him from the night before.

Or had that been the champagne?

Cameron was careful not to press her too far. The impatience he'd felt had been tamped. He'd been stunned by Julia's fierce response to him last night. He was certain she was as attracted to him as he was to her, and he was supremely confident that he would eventually have her. He was willing now to go slowly, certain that in the end she would come to him. For today he was content simply to be with her.

As they neared their destination Cam glanced sideways at Julie, then said levelly, "The Institute is one of my favorite havens."

Tension eased as she politely added her agreement that it was one of the finest museums in the country. By the time they passed the bronze lions that stood guard over the entrance to the building, they once again shared a companionable, if cautious, rapport.

Several young children proudly perched on the back of one of the lions while an equally proud parent recorded it for posterity with his camera. Cam's lips slid into a smile, and Julie matched it with a lighthearted one of her own. It was one of the last things they agreed on that afternoon.

Inside, Julia stared intently and reverently at the works of David, Van Gogh, and Rembrandt, while Cameron stared intently and irreverently at her. The fluidity of her movements enchanted him. The graceful poise of her stance enchanted him. The silken twining of amber, gold, and flaxen in her hair enchanted him. She enchanted him.

Aware of his regard, Julie unconsciously softened. Her smile became more alluring, her expressions more inviting. It had been a long time since a man had looked at her the way Cameron did, and she responded like a flower turning to the rain after a drought. She knew it was dangerous to encourage him, and yet, that knowledge added to her mounting pleasure.

When they came to a painting by Rubens, Cam pursed his lips in a silent whistle over the well-rounded nude.

"Now, that's what I call a woman," he said with a wolfish leer. "Plump and juicy."

"You sound like you're talking about a piece of chicken," Julia reproved.

"That's right. Finger-lickin' good," he agreed in a lascivious whisper. She looked down her long nose at him, so he added mischievously, "You're just jealous because you know Rubens would've turned up his nose if *you'd* applied to model."

She laughed in light agreement, but felt a pricking deep within. As they strolled on she couldn't resist looking back over her shoulder at the voluptuous beauty whose alluring charms Rubens had depicted so well. Julie had the sinking notion that Cam's taste in women paralleled that of Rubens. More than ever she believed she was simply a game to him, a challenging prey to be stalked and captured.

And once caught?

The answer was depressingly clear.

Her enjoyment was diminished; she viewed painting after painting without seeing what was before her. Cam sensed her withdrawal and felt a sense of pique. Dammit, where did the real Julie go when this plain, prim woman appeared?

He started speaking about the merits of each painting, keeping up an inconsequential flow of talk without expecting a response. By the time they came to view the works of modern artists like Picasso, Klee, and Calder, he knew she'd begun to relax and his own tension eased. Standing before one of Pollock's splattered spectrals, he noted Julia's wrinkled nose and laughed out loud.

"I should have known you wouldn't appreciate abstract expressionism," he said with a shake of his head.

"Oh? And why is that?"

"You're too precise, that's why. You like everything exact and defined, detailed and categorized. You want paintings to reflect what you see, not what you feel. Feelings make you uncomfortable, don't they, Julie?" He sent a shrewd glance over her that made her shiver. "Feelings aren't clear-cut, and you don't like that. There's no room for ambiguity in your life."

You want ambiguity? You should look in my heart, she thought, but all she said was, "Well, I would have known you'd prefer this sort of thing." She nodded to the Pollock painting. "This looks precisely like your room before the maid arrives."

"Touché," returned Cam with a quirking brow.

They turned, and Julie bumped into a man standing behind her; Cam quickly steadied her with a hand to her elbow. She felt his touch down to her toes. She looked in his eyes and saw her own shock mirrored there. Pulling her arm away from his hand, she stepped forward, her feet keeping pace to the sudden wild drumming of her heart.

They studied Grant Wood's *American Gothic,* and with an exchanged grin, mugged an imitation. They assiduously avoided touching, but each was aware of the warmth and texture of the other standing so near. They wandered into the Thorne Rooms, where Julie oohed and ahhed over more than sixty exquisitely detailed miniature rooms. She continually clapped her hands and pointed with the excitement of a child. Cam, hugely enjoying her delight, was sorry to move on. Eventually they strolled outside to argue over the Ferguson Fountain of the Great Lakes; she liked the quaint beauty of the five maidens who symbolized the spirit of each of the lakes, he preferred the more modern pool with three crowns of water on the north mall. And finally, surprised to find it was nearly six, they headed for a quiet supper at a small restaurant Cam insisted served the best seafood in town.

Over boiled shrimp and salads, they recounted the day, sharing an intimate laughter that was different and therefore undeniably stimulating. As Julia began to thaw, forgetting her earlier dejection, she began to speak about her childhood in a small South Dakota town; her love of the endless prairies and the unobscured skies. She spoke with odd affection of the sequestering blizzards in winter and the stultifying heat waves in summer. By the time coffee was served, she was completely caught up in her memories, her eyes as bright as the sky she described, her gestures vivid with animation. She paused, and Cameron watched her lips press against the glaze of her coffee mug. An envious longing surged through him, immobilizing him as he stared at her.

Sensing his sudden stillness, Julie laughed nervously. It was unlike her to reveal so much of herself, and she spoke quickly to cover her disquiet at having done so. "I'm sorry. I've monopolized the conversation with talk that must nominate me for Bore of the Year."

"You weren't boring at all," he contradicted. He regarded his coffee with the look of one beholding a mysterious treasure. He began to toy with his spoon, spinning it lightly this way, then that. "I wish I'd had a childhood like yours, with lazy summers and isolated winters. I grew up near L.A. We had one season—smog. And it was filled with a never-ending hustle and bustle."

Julie watched his long fingers wind around the spoon and was jolted by the memory of his touch. A ridiculous resentment of the spoon leaped up, and she ruthlessly thrust it aside. "Tell me about it," she urged him, anxious to erase the disturbing image of his caressing fingers.

"Not much to tell," he said with a shrug. But she fixed her blue eyes on him so expectantly, he began to talk. He opened up to her in a way he never had to anyone. He told her about growing up in California, about attending college at Berkeley in the volatile years of the early seventies, about accidentally landing a job with Galaxy Records right out of college. They ordered wine, and at her calm prodding he spoke of his younger brother, Chad; his sister-in-law, Doris; and his nieces, Katie and Anne.

"What about your parents?" asked Julie. She wanted him to go on talking. She wanted to know everything about him. She wanted to know who he was and why.

But at her question Cam's face closed, and he blatantly checked his watch. "We really should be going, Julie. Do you realize we've been here over three hours?"

She tilted her head, studying the thin line of his lips, the cloud dulling his eyes. He was reaching for the check. Leaning forward, she laid her hand over his, stilling his motion.

"Did something happen to your parents?" Her voice was matter-of-fact, seemingly void of the worry, the sympathy she felt rising within her.

Cameron gazed fixedly at the slim hand covering his. Her lightest touch had a power over him he found impossible to deny. Slowly, unwillingly, he continued in a monotone. "I was six; Chad nearly three. I went off to school one day and came home to find I no longer had a mother."

He spoke without expression, but Julia did not doubt the depth of his bitterness. "What happened?"

"Mother was a trend-setter. She was a runaway wife before it became popular. She took one suitcase full of clothes and nothing else. Not even a picture to remember us by. We never heard from her again."

It explained so much. His feelings toward women and marriage—and her. Julia pictured him as that small boy, deserted and scared, and ached to hold him, to soothe him, to somehow wash away his bitter hurt. She sat motionless, waiting patiently.

He withdrew his hand from beneath hers and continued in controlled tones. "My father took in a succession of girl friends, none of whom wanted to be saddled with two small boys. Four years later he finally got a divorce and married his current live-in. She reluctantly agreed to keep one of us. Chad stayed. I was farmed out to an aunt. About every two years I was sent on to stay with a different relative. As soon as I was old enough, I moved out to live on my own."

He looked at her then. His lips twisted in a crooked smile that touched Julie more deeply than any of his more charming displays. "End of story. God knows why I even told you about it. It beats you out for Bore of the Year, hands down."

She shook her head wordlessly. Her hair fanned out, radiant wings in the subdued lighting of the restaurant. Watching her, his mouth settled into his usual easy smile. "My father, by the way, is now on his fifth—or maybe sixth, I'm not sure which—marriage. I've seen him a couple of times, but we can't really find much to say to each other these days."

"Cameron," said Julia softly. "Let's go home."

As he picked up the check she smiled, and he wanted to hold her so badly, his hands shook.

CHAPTER SEVEN

He'd said he'd use whatever weapon necessary to win her and it was readily apparent his arsenal was well stocked.

The charming smile, the heated glance, the brief blazing touch —Cameron had them all, and he used them to deadly effect. If they were doing dishes, he stood within a breath of her, his thigh occasionally grazing hers, but never pressing upon her enough to warrant an objection. If they were reading the evening paper, he stared at her straight through the printed page. If they were simply passing each other in the corridor, he infused the air with his desire in one heart-stopping smile.

Even a friendly game of backgammon became as charged as the flashiest video-game match-up. Attempting to move her counters, Julie would bump into Cam's hand as it accidentally lingered over the board. She'd reach for the dice and brush into his fingers; she'd look up from a roll to find him staring intently at her. By game's end, she'd feel as if she'd been hit with fifty volts of electricity.

Working late at the shop and heading straight for bed offered little protection. Several times in the last two weeks he'd materialized with her morning coffee. Twice he'd strolled in, exuding a fresh clean smell and wearing nothing but a towel draped loosely around his hips. The sight of him like that sent Julia scurrying to the safety of her bookshop, but nothing could dispel it from her mind.

She didn't even have to see him to know when he walked into

the room. Her skin would tingle, and her pulse would almost sound out the message with a racing beat. It seemed there was nothing about him she wasn't aware of. She could have easily recounted the number of breaths he drew in any given moment. She knew to a millimeter how far his lips uptilted when he grinned and how far his eyelids dropped when he gazed at her. She pretended to ignore his melting smiles and searing looks, but at night, alone in her bed, she would remember them and twist and turn with an aching need she refused to yield to.

Julia asked herself daily why she didn't just give in and enjoy it while it lasted. The answer was always the same: She was afraid. Afraid of the crushing pain of rejection.

She'd read an article once that said the average woman recovered from a broken heart in six months to a year. Julie knew she wasn't average. She was only now overcoming the effects of her relationship with Allen, a relationship she was beginning to realize hadn't come close to being meaningful. She feared the emotional devastation of caring too much for Cameron Stone.

Grams had often said she was "a deep one, hard to reach." Julia was afraid of the depths of her feelings for Cam. She knew he was capable of hurting her far more than Allen ever had. She was becoming dependent on him, and this dependency frightened her.

Finally, desperate to talk to someone, Julia began confiding in Mary Beth. She explained her fears, telling her—without realizing it—how endearing, how maddening, how essential Cameron had become to her.

Mary Beth listened intently and never once said, "You sound like a woman in love." Instead, she said, "If living with Cam causes you such turmoil, why not move out?"

Julie busied herself with wrapping up several books to be mailed out that afternoon. She refused to meet M.B.'s steady gaze. "Because I *like* living with him. I wasn't meant to live alone, Mary Beth. I hated it. As aggravating as he is, it's fun to be with Cam."

"Maybe it could be even more fun," suggested M.B. dryly as she handed Julie a pair of scissors.

Snipping her words as precisely as she snipped a length of strapping tape, Julie vehemently denied this. "Has Cam paid you to convince me for him?" she inquired icily.

"I just think it's time for you to open up, Jules." Mary Beth swung her frizzy black curls emphatically and produced the ultimate argument. "Greg thinks so too. He says you need to fall in love."

"I don't need the pain a love affair could bring," she declared in a fierce whisper. She smiled weakly at a customer who glanced up in curiosity, then continued more calmly. "I've been through one love affair, and this is a far superior arrangement. This way," she finished in a firm voice meant to be convincing, "I have the companionship without the complications."

Mary Beth issued a snort of disbelief and shot behind the safety of a high stack of books.

The conversation was not mentioned again, but it continued to whirl around Julia's head. Was she a Sleeping Beauty, needing to be awakened? Did she need Cam?

She didn't *want* to need him.

They were such opposites in outlook, habits, life-styles. There wasn't the least possibility of making anything last between them. Not that Cam had ever indicated he desired anything permanent. Since the day at the Art Institute she could understand this. Understanding what lay behind Cameron's attitude toward commitment, however, didn't change Julia's attitude toward it. It remained as necessary to her as it was meaningless to him.

Long after M.B. left, Julie lingered, wrapping up books that had been ordered from their spring catalog and preparing them for shipment. Not even to herself would she admit that she was loath to spend another long night alone with Cameron, restlessly yearning and fearing. She had, she continually said to herself, so much work to do.

Occasionally she would pause in the middle of taping a box to stare into space, envisioning Cam sprawled out on the study sofa, scattering sections of the newspaper as he read, or in the kitchen, cheerfully ordering her from one chore to the next. When she imagined herself beside him, Julie would impatiently shake the visions away. She shied from giving shape to her desires.

It was well past nine when she decided she couldn't put off going home any longer. Resolutely she shrugged into her leather jacket, wondering why Cam hadn't called to check on her. Usually when she didn't walk through the door at six-fifteen, he was calling the shop at six-sixteen. Perhaps he'd needed a night of solitude too.

A faint drumming could be heard in the carports. Julia eased her rust-speckled Toyota into the slot beside Cam's silver Jag and sat for several minutes before turning off the ignition, trying to determine the source of the sound. Finally she got out and crossed the parking lot, her shoes crunching into the gravel. As she came round the side of the building she knew with a sinking heart that the noise was coming from her own apartment.

The foyer reverberated with the blare and thump of overloud music. It surprised Julie, for Cam had made a conscious effort to keep the volume of his music turned down. The front door was unlocked. As she pushed it open a blast of rock 'n' roll hit her fully. She stared open-mouthed at the people who seemed to carpet the living room from wall to wall. Women in long sleek gowns that dipped precariously low laughed in shrill excitement. Men in a mélange of formal suits and faded denims lounged with studied ease.

A boisterous foursome came up behind her and carried her into the press of people. Feeling like Alice dropped into Wonderland, Julia stood uncertainly amid the incessant babble of voices clashing with the continually raucous music. The pungent aroma of an illegal substance interwoven with stale cigarette smoke permeated the air. Instant images of herself being locked behind steel bars rose hazily with the clouds of smoke. Julie shut her eyes, hoping the vision—and the reality—would disappear.

Realizing she was being both foolish and cowardly, Julia squinted her eyes and looked around. She saw several people casting cursory glances over her, evaluating and dismissing her in the blink of an eye. She knew she must have looked like a frump in her frayed jacket and shirtwaist khaki dress. Compared to these oh-so-fashionably smart trend-setters, she could easily have been mistaken for the cleaning woman.

Her temper began to rise. How could Cameron do this? How could he throw a party like this and not even *warn* her?

A thin young man with colorless hair that had apparently never seen a comb sloshed liquor over her sleeve. He muttered, "Sorry, darling," and pushed past her without so much as a downward glance. A woman following him trounced Julie's toe with a lethally spiked heel.

She would kill him. She vigorously rubbed her damp sleeve with her hand and her injured toe along her calf. She would kill him *if* she could find him. Squeezing between a back and a protruding stomach, she searched angrily for Cam. The man with the stomach proffered what looked like a badly rolled cigarette at her.

"Wanna hit?" he yelled into her ear.

She shook her head and decided burning Cam alive would be too good for him. The heavy man shrugged and turned to offer the joint to someone else.

That was when she saw him.

He stood several feet away in the center of an admiring circle. The brief glimpse of him rattled Julie's breath in her lungs. A steel-gray suit and tight black turtleneck showcased his dark good looks with sophistication. He appeared taller, stronger, more polished than she'd ever seen him. It was obvious Cam was in his element. He fit in. She did not.

She watched with mounting resentment as he tipped his head to bestow a broad smile on someone beside him. Julia craned her neck to peer around the nearly naked back of the woman with the deadly shoe. She instantly wished she hadn't. The recipient of Cam's smile was a striking beauty whose startling strand of white streaking through her flowing raven tresses set her off from everyone else in the crowd. Which was, thought Julie dejectedly, no mean feat.

Cam threw his arm about the woman's bare shoulders and a nauseated feeling instantly swept through Julie. The woman's voluptuous figure appeared ready at any moment to pop from her shimmery metallic gown. The Rubens nude came to Julia's mind. She knew this was the kind of woman to make Cam smack his lips. Pure, bright green envy flooded her. To look that gorgeous in a crowd like this! She suddenly felt inadequate, unable to measure up to the women around her.

She caught herself up short. How dare he make her feel this way! And in her own home! On a spurt of defensive animosity Julie roughly shoved herself forward.

"Good evening, Cameron," she said, producing a saccharine-laced tone. Her mouth curved in an equally sweet smile, but her eyes glinted pure arsenic. "I do believe we've run out of guacamole dip, my dear. Do you think you could help me find some in the kitchen?"

She wheeled without looking to see if he followed. He did. Threading her way through what seemed to be an endless procession of bodies that were encamped along the length of their apartment, Julia made her way to the brightly lighted kitchen. Though music still resounded deafeningly, it seemed blessedly quiet compared to the overstuffed atmosphere of the living room. Julie braced herself against the sink and rounded on Cam.

"Who are all these people?" she hissed.

He shrugged. "Friends of mine."

"Friends!" she shrieked. Seeing several heads turn her way, all eyeing the two of them curiously, she lowered her voice to a furious whisper. "What's going on here?"

Cameron looked around with interest. Bringing his gaze back

to Julia's anger-reddened face, he said calmly, "I'd say it's a party."

"A party!" Her voice rose again. "This is more like a convention!"

He smiled widely, and it was only with a tremendous effort that Julie kept from stamping her foot. "I don't think it's very considerate of you to invite all these people without at least telling me about it," she seethed. "This was a very unpleasant surprise after a long workday."

"I'm sorry, Julie," said Cam. He presented one of his most beguiling smiles. He saw she wasn't buying it and tried again. "I didn't plan this. Really. It more or less just happened. A few friends suggested we get together, and the next thing I knew, we were having a party."

She looked skeptical and unforgiving. "You could have called to let me know."

"I'm sorry. I didn't mean to upset you." He wanted to explain, but couldn't. He couldn't say, *I couldn't take another night alone with you, wanting you.* He couldn't say, *Being alone with you is slow sweet torture.* He couldn't say, *You're driving me mad, and I don't know what to do about it.*

"What do you intend to do?" she asked, somewhat more calmly.

"Do?" he repeated blankly.

"Yes, about this!" Julie flung out an arm to indicate the sea of people flowing in and out of the kitchen.

"Be reasonable, Julia. You can't expect me to ask everyone to go home, now can you?"

That was precisely what Julia did expect. She'd put in eleven hours at the shop and had expected to plop immediately into bed. Walking into a party the likes of which she'd never before seen had outraged her. But she couldn't resist the warm plea in Cam's melting brown eyes nor the silky caress in his voice.

With a sigh she grudgingly agreed. "I guess not."

He rewarded her with a dazzlingly crooked grin. "Now, why

don't you join the fun? There's some friends here I'd like you to meet."

Like that vamp you were draped all over? she wondered, then asked herself why did she care anyway? As for having fun, that was out of the question. Not at this party. She shook her head. "This isn't my kind of crowd, Cam. I'll just slip into my room and—"

"No way," he said, reaching to take hold of her arm.

Julie skittered back just as Cam was jostled by a tall broad man with neatly trimmed black hair. He turned and momentarily forgot her. "Danetti! What are you doing here?"

"Trying to find you," replied the dark man with a wide smile on his full lips. "I was beginning to think you hadn't attended your own party. But I saw Serena and knew you had to be somewhere close by."

That was as much as Julie heard before she faded quietly from the room. She had no doubt that Serena was the dramatic brunette she'd first seen with Cam. Humph! Serena was welcome to him, thought Julie as she stamped into her bedroom. She flicked on the light and stared in shock at the half-dressed couple on her bed.

"Hey! What's the deal? Go away!" said the male.

"Kindly get out of my bedroom," said Julia through her teeth. "Or I shall call the police and have you thrown out."

They dithered only a moment. The look on Julie's face told them she meant every word she uttered. While they scrambled to dress and leave in haste, Julie stood rigidly by the door. She held it open for them when they departed and slammed it shut after them. She glared at the mussed state of her bed. Cameron would have a lot to answer for in the morning.

She stormed to the bed and straightened it in a few swift, short jerks. It made her feel ill to think of strangers writhing on it. Without warning, her mind filled with visions of Cameron and the stunning Serena, half clothed, writhing together. She stiffened and stood staring accusingly at her bed for several seconds.

Whirling, Julia threw open her closet and hurled her jacket onto a hanger. She rummaged at the back, finally pulling free a long plastic bag. Laying this on the end of the bed, she sat beside it and picked up the phone, grateful that Cam had insisted she have her own private line. She dialed and listened to her heart banging between the rings.

"Hello," said M.B. in the middle of the fourth ring.

"Are you two busy? Do you have plans for the rest of the evening?" she asked, then continued on a rush. "Because if you're free, I'd like you to do me a favor."

Briefly she explained the situation while Mary Beth emitted sharp whistles. "What do you want us to do?" she inquired when Julie finished describing the party.

"I want you to come over and give me moral support. I've decided to join the fun, as Cam quaintly put it." The line was silent. Julie said timidly, "You will come, won't you?"

"Of course, we will!" declared M.B. "I wouldn't dream of missing it! We'll get there as soon as we can."

"Mary Beth, if you've got something slick, wear it. Greg can come however he pleases, but the women here are dazzling."

She began tossing off her shirtwaist the instant she hung up. Yanking the plastic from the hanger, she removed a shiny silk azure gown from its folds. This was her dress for special occasions. She shook it out and held the length of it pressed against her body. It was a simple draping of cloth, tied together at one shoulder while bare over the other. She hadn't worn it in more than a year and she hoped it would still fit as it should.

It did. The soft silk clung to her figure, shaping her firm, high breasts and rounding her hips. Whenever she moved, it glimmered like the northern lights and reflected the sparkling blue of her eyes. She wore no jewelry with it. After a moment's hesitation she swept her hair up into a very casual knot pinned carefully into place. When she'd donned matching blue heels and a light dusting of makeup, Julia cautiously peered around the edge of the door. Should she go out now or wait for Mary Beth and Greg to come get her?

The solution presented itself in the form of a sandy-haired mustached male who sighted her before she crept back into her room. He was at her side in an instant, forcing her to keep the door open while he smiled at her.

"Where have you been all my life?" he asked while taking inventory of the goods she had to offer.

"In my bedroom," she said coolly.

He looked over her shoulder, and his gleaming smile faded. "Are you Cameron's Julia?"

"No," she replied, restoring his smile. "I'm my own Julia."

The volatile smile disappeared again. "Just my luck," he said in tones of disgust.

He turned to leave, but she clamped a hand on his arm, stopping him. Any port in a storm, thought Julie. She wasn't going out into that mob alone. But if she waited any longer for the Farrows, she wasn't going to have the courage to go out there at all. She managed a wavering smile.

"Wait a minute," she said in a voice considerably warmer. "You have the advantage of knowing who I am. What's your name?"

For some reason her question surprised him. He searched her face intently, then said slowly, "Mike Rivers."

She held out her hand. "Hello, Mike."

He took it with a grin. "You don't know who I am, do you?" he said in a voice of near wonder.

"Should I?"

"Is this a lesson in humility? 'The rock star shalt not think too highly of himself?' Is that it?"

"Are you a rock star?" asked Julie in turn.

Mike laughed and put her hand through his arm. "I'll be whatever you want me to be," he said gallantly as he led her down the corridor.

To her relief he was both sober and sensible. He managed to

keep people from falling into her while satisfying the constant demands for his attention from passersby. Partygoers were going on to other parties, and the living room wasn't quite as crowded as before. Almost the instant they entered, Julia sighted Cam. He was standing by the fireplace between the man he'd called Danetti and the woman with the astonishing white streak in her hair.

As she came in with Mike Cam looked up, laughing. His laughter broke off as though severed with a well-honed blade. His eyes narrowed as they ran from tousled topknot to shiny blue toe, taking in every curve, every hollow, so well outlined in the azure silk. Seeing his intent stare, his companions also inspected her, assessing her as if she were about to be auctioned off. Julia began to wish she'd stayed in her room.

Cameron clapped his whiskey glass on the mantel, sending a spray of liquor over the carved edge. He smiled thinly at them as they drew nearer. His voice was clear and cold. "What the hell are you doing?"

Julie blinked at the barely suppressed anger in his voice. Surprise immediately gave way to satisfaction. She was glad to have annoyed him. This entire episode was annoying *her*! Her eyes skated past him to his friends. They were pretending not to see the hostile byplay between Cam and herself.

"I've come to meet your friends," she replied with a tranquillity she knew would further irritate him.

The music drowned the gnashing of his teeth. "Tony Danetti and Serena Seifert," he said with the curtest of nods to each.

"Hello, Julia. We've heard a lot about you," breathed Serena in a voice of smoke. "Hi, Mike," she added with a sensual parting of her crimson-lacquered lips. "How's the taping going?"

"Great," he answered. To Julie's dismay, he relinquished his hold on her. She'd never felt a greater need for physical support. But his hands waved expressively as he elaborated, "We've finished the rhythmics and the scratch vocals. We're aiming to wind it up by July."

"Are you in the business, too, Julia?" inquired the darkly handsome Tony.

"No," she replied. She infused her voice with what smoke she could, but she rather thought it was a mere wisp compared to Serena's dense smoldering. "I'm in the book business."

Breaking in on this exchange, Cam said tightly, "Oh, my, I see we're out of guacamole again. Perhaps, my dear, we should go get some."

He clenched her arm, cutting off circulation like a well-placed tourniquet, and hauled her away from the small circle before she could protest. She wrenched her arm free as soon as they were in the hall. She glared at him, then spun toward the kitchen. Her adrenaline was pumping, and her heart was pounding. What had made Cam look at her so furiously?

She was the one who should be looking furious! This surprise party had been sprung on her, not him. He had no excuse for glowering at her. Once in the kitchen she whirled on him and stated as coolly as she could, "I hope you're drunk, because I can see no other reasonable explanation for your behavior."

"What do you think you're doing?" he demanded hotly, ignoring her sarcasm.

"Doing? I'm doing what you told me to. Joining the fun."

"And just what is this?" he asked, flicking his finger over the strap crossing her shoulder. "Your hunting outfit?"

He'd gone mad. There was no other explanation. "Hunting?" she echoed weakly.

"For husbands," he said tersely.

"Don't be—"

"To think that for two months you've been dressing like a Salvation Army dowd—"

"I have not!"

"And tonight you suddenly turn into Cinderella. Well, your pumpkin has arrived, Cindy. Go change your clothes," he commanded between short sharp breaths.

She stared in speechless disbelief. His taut face was flushed with anger. He held his hands back as if he feared what he might do with them. The seams of the gray suit stretched to the breaking point over his rigidly set shoulders. Julie visualized those shoulders pressed so closely to Serena's, and she stiffened.

"You have no right to order me about," she objected.

"I'm not having you parade your wares for that bunch of lechers to ogle!" he bellowed.

Julie darted a glance past his shoulder. The crowd had thinned, but the few people passing through for drinks or ice paused to stare. He was going to create a scene, and inwardly Julie cringed. She tried to swallow her fury. Lowering her voice, she said in what she hoped were rational tones, "I'm not parading, Cam, and you really don't have any right to speak to me in this manner. Now, why don't we go back to your guests—"

"I am not arguing this with you any further. Get out of that dress, Julia, or I'll change your clothes myself. I'll talk to you about this in the morning."

"*You'll* talk to *me*!" she gasped, forgetting her abhorrence of a scene. "Oh, you insufferable, conceited—"

"Jules! We've been looking all over for you!" broke in a cheery voice. Mary Beth didn't let Cameron's scowl daunt her. She bounced in between the arguing couple, beaming smiles at them both and speaking in a gush of words. "I love your dress! You look simply stunning! Doesn't she, Greg? Tell me, do you think this is slick enough?"

She twirled around in a swish of flame-red crepe. The dress was cocktail-length, with belled sleeves and a scoop neck. It hugged her curvaceous form to a breath-stopping degree. Turning her smile upon Cam, she said gaily, "I'm Mary Beth, and this is Greg. I'm sure Julie's told you about us. She's certainly told us about you. I love the apartment. Show us around, will you, Julie?"

Julia let herself be hauled out of the room but not before delivering a parting shot. "I'm glad you like the dress, Mary

Beth," she said loudly. "Let me tell you what Mike Rivers had to say about it."

Moving into Julie's bedroom, Greg and M.B. spoke as one. "What's going on?" they demanded.

Picking up her hairbrush and setting it down again, Julie said distantly. "I don't know. Cam doesn't like my dress. He says I should change it. Actually he ordered me to change it."

"We heard. I think half the neighborhood heard," said Greg in his dry way.

"He had the look of a volcano about to erupt," remarked Mary Beth as she twisted to examine her curvy form in the mirror. She fluffed the puffy sleeves of her dress. "If you ask me, I'd say he was red-hot jealous."

"Jealous!" exclaimed Julie. "Don't be absurd. There's nothing between us to account for jealousy!" She firmly quashed the memory of her own earlier sickening flare of jealousy and added vehemently, "He's just bad-tempered."

"Is he always so dictatorial?" M.B. ran her hands over the folds of red crepe molded against her hip, but her eyes were on Julie's mirrored reflection.

A reluctant smile softened Julie's lips. "Sometimes." She fidgeted with some bobby pins lying on her dresser. "What do you think I should do?"

"Go out there and have a good time," said M.B. promptly. "You can't let him order you around. The dress looks terrific. And besides, Mike Rivers asked us to tell you to hurry back. I should only be so lucky!"

"Watch it," warned Greg. He winked at Julia from behind his wire rims and playfully yanked one of his wife's bobbing curls. "I'll order you home if you talk like that."

"Oh, men!" Mary Beth dismissed his threat with an airy wave of her squat hand. "You aren't going to hide in your room, Jules, and that's that. You simply couldn't be so selfish as to invite me here and then make me miss all the glitter and action!" She took Julia's arm and pulled her toward the door, throwing in the clinching argument, "What right has Cameron to tell you what to do? Come on, you have some partying to do!"

Julie didn't resist Mary Beth's insistent tugging. The more she thought about it, the angrier she got. What right did Cam have to dictate anything to her? He didn't want to be committed to her, but he didn't want her to find anyone else either. Well, if he could have his Serena Seiferts, she could certainly have a Mike Rivers or two!

When she rejoined the party, entering between the protective Farrows, Cam was conversing in low, silky tones with Serena. Julie pointedly ignored him. She skimmed gracefully to Mike, who cheerfully signed an autograph for Mary Beth, then stood listening to him compliment her without hearing a single word. His arm came around her, pulling her against his side, and still Julie remained unaware of him.

The oddest thoughts were whizzing through her mind. Today was Saturday, well, Sunday really. The cleaning maid came on Wednesdays. What was going to be done about this mess? Her eyes roved the array of empty bottles, tipped-over glasses, and overflowing ashtrays. A large stain spread over the carpet near her niche. A leaf had been knocked from her schefflera and lay tattered by the corner of the sofa.

Her gaze came full circle, back to the group near the fireplace. Just as she was noting the broken glass strewn over the mantel, she caught Cam's gaze. He eyed her with the look of one confronting a hair in his drink. Before she could react to it, Cameron slid his eyes quickly past her, as if the sight of her could not be tolerated.

That look, more than anything else about the entire disastrous evening, struck Julia to the core. How dare he look at her like that! How dare he dismiss her so contemptuously! She wanted to slap him, to scream abuses at him, to dash liquor over him. Instead, she smiled brightly at Mike Rivers, nodding and murmuring polite phrases that meant nothing at all. She caught occasional glimpses of M.B. and Greg clinging together and laughing gaily as they mingled with the elite crowd. Each time, a miserable stab of envy pierced her, but she told herself she was glad someone was enjoying the party.

When a bottle of tequila was suddenly passed into her hands, Julia looked at it in utter blankness. Mike laughed and suggested it was time she learn how to drink tequila straight. She was about to shake her head and politely refuse when her eyes once again met Cameron's. His gaze still conveyed all the warmth of a man eyeing a cockroach. Julia slid her eyes over the beautiful Serena and felt a renewal of her earlier inadequacy. Why couldn't she be like these people? Why couldn't she let herself go and just once forget propriety? It was obvious that men like Cam preferred a woman who was free of rigid principles. Why couldn't she ignore all those small-town mores Cam considered so old-fashioned? Well, why not?

With a defiant toss of her head Julie flashed a brilliant smile at Mike and agreed that it was indeed time.

He disappeared briefly, returning from the kitchen with a filled tray. Amid much laughter, Mike proceeded to teach Julie how to "shoot tequila." First he made her take a bite of lemon, then a lick of salt. Then he handed her a shot glass of tequila and told her to down it in one swift gulp. Julie let the shot of tequila burn a fast track down her throat. Then she doused the fire with the beer Mike thrust into her hand. After two demonstrations Julia forgot about Cameron's disapproving glares. After the third, catching him scowling at her, she stuck out her tongue, then giggled.

Three was all she had, but three was more than sufficient. The party became fuzzier and fuzzier. She knew she was having a good time, because she was laughing so much. She wasn't at all certain why she was laughing, but it was much better than feeling sorry for herself because Cameron would have nothing to do with her. At some point she realized that Mary Beth and Greg were gone. Then she discovered lights were being turned off and sounds had dimmed. She felt herself being carried in strong arms and mumbled a blurry thanks to Mike for being so sweet as to put her to bed.

It didn't occur to her to object to being undressed by her benefactor. She simply snuggled into the cool sheets and went instantly to sleep.

CHAPTER EIGHT

Julia gradually became aware of the rancid taste in her mouth. She tried to move her tongue, but it seemed weighted with lead. As if to escape the unpleasant taste she rolled onto her side. She was instantly aware that she was completely naked. No nightgown, no underwear, nothing. Just Julie between the sheets. Feeling incredibly decadent, she kicked her legs experimentally.

She bumped into warm flesh.

Her heart stilled. Not daring to look, Julia inched her leg backward. She rubbed against a leg that was long and hard and covered with hair. Her eyes flew open.

Cameron smiled lazily. He was lying on his side, propped up on an elbow, watching her from beneath half-drooped lids.

"Mornin'," he said softly.

If he'd shouted, he couldn't have extracted a more frenzied reaction. With a smothered shriek Julie sat up, realized her nakedness, and screeched in earnest as she frantically clasped the sheet to her breast. She slid to the edge of the bed and stared at him in horror.

Wrinkles of sleep crisscrossed one cheek and arm, bestowing him with an innocence belied by the sensuality in his eyes. His ruffled brown hair fell boyishly over his brow, contrasting with the manliness of his bare chest. *Was the rest of him naked too?* Julia wondered. Her pulse accelerated rapidly at the mere thought.

"What are you doing in my bed?" she demanded sharply.

His smile broadened. "But I'm not in your bed," he said with maddening calm. He waved his hand into the air. "You, my dear delight, are in mine."

Her eyes raced about the room, taking in the unfamiliar plain furnishings, and landed at the sight of herself reflected in the full-length beveled mirror on the door opposite the bed. It had to be a ghastly nightmare. It couldn't be real. Not this horribly rumpled blonde clutching the vivid damson sheet to her naked bosom as the tousled man beside her looked on in amusement. Intimate amusement.

Julie's tongue felt thicker than ever. She forced it to move over her dry lips. "What . . .? That is, did—did we . . .?"

Cam shifted. He stretched out his hand and sent a feathery fingertip up her bare spine. "Now, darling, what do you think?" he asked in a tone so suggestive, Julie had not the least doubt about what they had done.

He lay back against the pillow, smiling and tracing swirls on her back with his fingertip. She shivered and edged away from his touch. How could she have done this? Why, oh why, had she ever touched that tequila?

She moaned, and he instantly became all concern. "Does your head hurt? I'll fix you up with Doc Stone's restorative and some dry toast. You stay here and—"

"No!" she cut in. She stared at him, feeling an overwhelming urge to cry. She didn't remember it. She didn't remember making love to him, and she was certain she should. Why didn't she? All she remembered was Mike and the tequila and Mike carrying her to bed. . . .

"I thought you were Mike," she said flatly.

His smile vanished. His brows clamped together. "Disappointed?" he inquired in a voice that was a sneer.

Disappointed! How could she be? She didn't even remember! And now she'd somehow upset him! Her hair spilled forward as she bent her head. She nervously plaited the sheet through her fingers, trying to sort out what had happened the night before and what it all meant today. Her brain seemed clogged, and she couldn't get the gears unstuck.

She peeked at him through the veil of her hair. He was frowning, the lines of his face set coldly against her. How could he look at her like that after being so gentle and loving when she'd first awakened? A dark stain was seeping over his face, and she wondered miserably what it signified. Anger? Disappointment? What? She couldn't guess. With a sinking feeling she realized that she hardly knew him.

They were strangers. Despite the month they'd shared the apartment, they were still strangers. Their schedules often kept them apart, and even when they were together, they'd only opened up to each other in small degrees. She didn't know his favorite color or his middle name. She didn't even know his birthday! She suspected he was thirty-three or -four, but she didn't *know*. How could she have made love to a man she really didn't know?

Unconsciously her clutch on the sheet tightened, and her head bowed lower. The morning light washed over her, bathing her delicate skin with an ethereal translucence and her hair with a radiant halo. To Cameron she was a moment of defenseless beauty, like a raindrop caught in a spider's web. His anger faded in his desire to capture that beauty.

"My love," said Cam, startling her. "Why don't you just lie back, and I'll massage away your troubles."

Her head whipped up, and her eyes filled with alarm. What she needed was to be alone—away from his distracting influence. "No! I—I need to—to go to the bathroom," she said hurriedly. She cast a wild eye at the door, then at Cam. He was clearly enjoying the situation. She slew him with a glare and requested coldly, "Could you please bring me a wrap?"

He chuckled and rose from the bed so swiftly, she scarcely had time to avert her eyes. She'd briefly seen the raw length of his legs, the rippling muscles of his buttocks, proving beyond doubt what had occurred the night before. Guilt washed over her in floodtides. Worse, she felt weighted with depression because she couldn't remember it. What kind of a woman made love to a man and didn't even remember it?

He dropped a short velour robe in her lap. She kept her eyes closed, listening intently for his departure. Hearing nothing, she chanced a peek and immediately shut her eyes again. My God, he was fit! She hadn't seen an ounce of fat anywhere on his body. Not that she'd taken time to inspect it, of course. But she couldn't help noticing the shape of him when he stood directly between her and the door, apparently waiting for her to don the robe. Julia clasped the maroon velour to her bosom as though raising a shield on a battlefield.

"Could you please . . .? Would you mind?" she asked in muffled distress.

"After having slept with me without a stitch on, what's the sense in being modest now?" he inquired reasonably.

"If you can't be a gentleman . . ." she mumbled into the sheet. She slipped beneath the covers, pulling the robe in with her and after twisting in unladylike contortions, she managed to fold the velour around her. It was much too large, of course, and lamentably lacked buttons, but at least it saved her from the indignity of further displaying herself to him. With a deep breath of courage she flung back the covers and dashed to the door with her eyes squeezed shut. She listened to his laughter all the way down that long, long corridor.

She grabbed clothes without looking at them and locked herself into the safety of her bathroom. Someone had retched with little accuracy into her toilet. This was decidedly the worst nightmare she'd ever fallen into. The problem was, how to get out of it?

After downing three aspirins, Julie cleaned the mess and jumped into the hottest shower she'd ever run. She wanted to cleanse away her problems, to send her hangover down the drain along with her guilty conscience. Most of all, she wanted to wash away the image of Cam as he'd stood naked before her. She tried to remember the feel of that naked body against hers and couldn't. She tried to imagine it and trembled at the weakness she felt at the thought.

Shaking her head beneath the spray of steaming water, Julie attempted to clear out the cobwebs. What, after all, had happened? So they'd gone to bed. Why should that change anything?

Because, she answered ruefully, it had already changed everything. But perhaps it would be for the better. Perhaps M.B. had been right, and things could be even more fun now.

Out of the mist arose a vision of black hair dramatically streaked with white. Julie waved her hand through the steam cloud, dispelling the misty mirage. Fun for how long, she wondered bitterly. Until the next party? What had happened to the striking Serena? Would Cam discard her just as quickly someday in favor of another? She immediately asked herself why she should worry about it. Why not enjoy the here and now and ignore the future?

Because, drummed the water into her ears, *you love him.*

She had been stupid enough to fall in love with Cameron.

By the time Julia had powdered, brushed her teeth, and dressed, she knew she had to leave. She couldn't change what had happened, but she could leave before her cracked heart shattered completely. The shocked remorse she'd felt since discovering herself in Cam's bed transformed into a furious resolve. She would not permit him to break her heart!

Without thinking coherently, simply intent on implementing her immediete departure, Julie rushed into the kitchen. It was a disaster area of spilled liquor; spoiled hors d'oeuvres; and scattered cans, bottles, and glasses. Ashes and cigarette stubs were dotted throughout, adding to the stale odor permeating the room. The maid, thought Julie, would take one look at this and quit on the spot. Well, it wouldn't be her problem.

Julia snatched a paper bag from beneath the sink and yanked out the bottom of the oven. She began tossing pots and pans into the sack with an indiscriminate clatter. She was adding a spatula and egg beater from a drawer when Cameron came in demanding to know what the hell was going on.

"I'm leaving," she replied tersely.

He watched her throw open a cupboard door, strewing cleansers and soap bottles onto the floor. "What?" he asked in blatant disbelief.

"I'm leaving," she repeated as she pulled out a scrubbing brush and dumped it in the bag.

"Why?"

"Isn't it obvious? I can't stay after last night."

Without glancing at him, she swept to the narrow pantry and started scooping armfuls of canned goods on top of the pans. Her hair hung in darkened wet clumps that whisked against her pale cheeks as she moved. Her plaid blouse had been misbuttoned in haste and was askew upon her slim frame. Her navy slacks were too large in the waist and kept slipping down over her hips. Cam watched her with enjoyment. He wasn't panicked. She was probably still more than a little tipsy—he could talk her out of this.

"Julie, be reasonable," he said calmly. "What's the big deal?"

Then she looked at him. He wore a pair of jeans and a freshly scrubbed look. She turned her eyes away from the sight of his bared chest, down to his bare feet. Nothing was going to stop her from leaving before it was too late. She crossed back to the sink to get another bag. He stepped in front of her and took her arm.

"It was inevitable, Julie. Surely you realize that. We can still go on living together, only now we can really enjoy it!"

"Will you get out of my way?" she demanded in quiet anger.

Instead of complying, Cam merely kicked the cupboard shut. "I'll make us some coffee and we can talk this over."

"There is nothing to talk about." Julia spun round and sprinted into her room. Cameron was right behind her. She lifted her suitcase from the closet shelf and carried it to the bed. He followed her step for step. She pitched the suitcase open and whirled only to crash into his chest.

Her palms pressed into his skin, and Julie heard her own sharp intake of breath echoed by his. She pulled her hands away and tried to sidestep him. He easily circumvented her. She began shaking with rage.

"Move out of my way!" she snapped.

"I don't understand why you're so upset," he told her, still [illegible] remain calm. "After last night there's no longer any need for us to hold back—"

"There's no longer any need for me to stay!" countered Julie.

"Julie," he began, but never finished as she shoved him aside. He tipped her suitcase shut with the flat of his palm and watched as she jerked a drawer out of the dresser and grabbed an armful of lingerie.

Racing back to the case on the bed, she found it closed. She flung it back open and hurled the clothes in. Cameron took them out and dumped them on the bed. She returned with a second load. She put them in; he instantly removed them. She brought a pile of sweaters and haphazardly dropped them into the empty suitcase. He picked them up.

"Will you stop it?" she asked through gritted teeth.

"You're not going anywhere until we've talked this out," said Cameron harshly. He was beginning to lose his temper. She was acting like an escapee from a lunatic asylum.

"I've told you, we have nothing to talk about." She grabbed for the sweaters, which he held away from her grasp.

"For the last time, Julia, you're not moving out," he stated with determination.

"No? Try and stop me!" She threw out the challenge as she whirled to retreat.

Sweaters flew in all directions as he lunged forward. Clamping his hands on her arms, he jerked her to a halt as if she were a puppet on a short string. "Okay! Go ahead and leave! I can't wait for you to go! God, I've never met such a prude!"

He was yelling now. And Julia, who had never yelled at anyone in her life, shouted back, "I am not!"

"Yes, you are! And frigid! You're a cold, frigid prude!" He

shook her with each word. Abruptly he ceased rattling her. He stood staring down at her as if she were the first woman he'd ever seen. Beneath the force of that gaze Julie's knees went weak. She stumbled within his hold and his grip tightened to catch her.

And then he was kissing her. His lips were in her hair, on [illegible] temple, over her ear, down her jaw. His hands were [illegible] over her slender back, pressing her forward into his hardening body. Cameron hadn't meant to start holding her, touching her, kissing her. But now that he was, he meant to continue until she responded as he knew she could. Until she was breathless with need for him. Until she was, at long last, his.

Later Julia decided she'd still been slightly drunk. The frenzied dash through the apartment, the hysterical packing, the shouting and the submission all indicated as much. The rationalization especially eased her conscience over the submission. For she'd scarcely resisted when Cam began devouring her. How could she resist? It seemed she'd waited a lifetime to taste again the magic of his kiss.

When his mouth at last covered hers, Julie met his kiss eagerly, passionately. She let her hands slide over his naked chest, marveling over the changing textures of his skin from smooth and soft to hard and firm, from downy here to grainy there. And all the while she wondered if this were how it had felt the night before. She longed desperately to know what it had been like.

As the kisses between them deepened, a voice said to her *Well, why not find out?* Julia was stunned. But if they'd already been intimate . . .

She swayed against him, touching his lips with her darting tongue, teasing and tantalizing.

"Don't kiss me like that if you don't mean it," he said with evaporating control.

"I mean it," she whispered into the ear she'd begun nibbling.

He went still, utterly motionless. She felt him tense from head to toe. Then he drew a long ragged breath and scooped her into his arms. She pressed herself against him and clung tightly to his neck.

This time she would remember. She would remember every breath, every heartbeat they shared.

They crumpled on top of the underthings spread over her bed. He pinned Julie to the mattress with his weight and lightly caught hold of the gilt threads weaving into her drying hair. He kissed her with fierce possession, knowing as he did so that the possessor would become the possessed. At length he pulled back to let her see all the hungry need, all the incalescent desire she evoked in him. In turn he saw the melting acceptance in her gaze, and he felt his body tighten with a passion that far surpassed any he'd ever known.

"I'm going to love you till the cows come home," he declared in thickened tones.

Julie's tremor of excitement shook the bed, jarring the suitcase shut. Cam knocked it to the floor, where it landed with a thump that echoed the thud of his heart. He hurled a rainbow of lingerie after it. Then he held himself slightly above her, still not daring to believe she wasn't going to dart away at any moment. He wanted her so badly, he thought he'd burst with the need.

Beneath him, the weight of his body suspended a breath from her, Julie felt her blood cascade through her veins. She was dizzy with the anticipation; she no longer cared whether or not he loved her, whether or not he'd break her heart. Her need for him throbbed so intensely, she thought she would explode. She willed him to hurry and suffered a savage delight when he did not.

Slowly he brought his hands to her blouse and began inching downward. Button by button he kissed the soft, scented flesh he exposed. In her rush to escape Julie hadn't put on a bra. When Cam gently spread her blouse open, his moan of pleasure sent a wave of hot breath over her breasts. He flicked his tongue over one pink puckered nipple. How could he have ever thought her less than perfect?

As he kissed her breast Julie sighed with the pleasure of it. She set her fingers against the planes of his face and touched as he touched, with exquisitely light, tantalizing brevity. Her fingertips danced downward to the nape of his neck, the spread of his shoulders. The flexing of his muscles delighted her, excited her. She savored the movement of him and moaned.

Cameron had to struggle to restrain himself from shredding her clothes and crashing into her. He forced himself to pull away. Julia's half-closed eyes widened, revealing liquid pools of love. "Cam?" she whispered.

He bent and dropped a kiss on her brow. "I'm not going anywhere without you," he said huskily. He stood up swiftly. His gaze held hers as he discarded his clothes. Then he leaned forward and with a gentle tug, removed the last of hers.

Her breasts rose and fell hurriedly. Her hair splayed over the pillow in a golden fan. She lay without moving and watched Cameron finish undressing her. She watched and wondered and wanted with an eagerness she'd never have believed possible.

"Wherever I go, I'm taking you with me," he said as he pressed back onto the bed. He moved over her and began once again the teasing loveplay that aroused them both to a pulsating peak.

It came as a shock to Julie that lovemaking could be more than an athletic exercise. As Cam caressed her with his hands, his lips, his breath, the sensations were so pleasurable, they were nearly unbearable. The need to return such sweet excitement filled her. She began responding with ardor, kissing and touching, darting her fingers over his back, his thighs, his buttocks, then lingering a moment before racing upward again. And as she gave and received, her desire for him spiraled.

Cam had had all kinds of women—shy and aggressive, cool and hot, innocent and experienced. Julie was all of these and none of these. His fingertips explored the fine structure of her bones, the delicate texture of her skin, the silken softness of her hair. She was softer, lovelier, warmer than any woman he'd ever known.

He burrowed his face into her long, lovely neck and told her on a ragged breath how good she felt, how much she excited him. And then at last he drove into her. He'd meant to take her slowly, drawing out each pleasure to its ultimate height. But he could no longer restrain himself. His thirst for her had to be slaked; he quenched it with hot, piercing thrusts that satisfied even as they drained.

Julie met his passionate demands with a swaying delirium of her own. As his hot flesh melted into hers, she pulsed with an agonizing intensity. This was the fulfillment she'd secretly craved since the day they met. When he shuddered into stillness, she slid into a lazy contentment. She felt sleepily sated . . . and profoundly in love.

He lay within her, never wanting to let her go. She tickled his ear with her tongue, then nipped. She blew a wisp of a laugh when he lifted his head to gaze drowsily at her.

"What a way to cure a hangover," she told him.

Her humor astonished him—and pleased him intensely. There was no vestige of the prim Julia in this beautiful woman smiling seductively at him. He kissed her nose, then said, "There is a streak of the wanton in you, m'dear, which I do believe must be thoroughly explored."

"Oh? By whom?" Julie lowered her lashes and breathily pursed her lips.

"Not only a wanton, but a tease as well!" He kissed the lips she so willingly presented.

"Was I teasing?"

He traced circles around her firm nipples with his thumb. "You'd better hope you were."

She sucked in a breath at the delight of his touch, then blew it out against his cheek. This was a delicious game she wanted never to end. Without meaning anything in particular, she taunted lightly, "Maybe I was, maybe I wasn't."

"If you so much as blink an eye at Mike Rivers again"—Cam set a kiss at each of the corners of her mouth—"or any other man

. . ." He deftly flicked his tongue over the curve of her lips. "I'll be forced to take extreme measures." He smothered her protest with a kiss of escalating passion.

She felt him stirring within her, felt her own pulses quivering anew. But his reference to Mike reminded her of last night, of Serena. She tamped down her mounting desires. If she let this go on, this is the way it always would be. Her pleasure dimmed by the constant doubt: When would he be leaving her? She couldn't bear to go through it, and she willed herself to stop while she still had a chance. Though her body still responded to his magical fingertips, her soul was withdrawing. She felt him tense slightly and knew he sensed something was wrong. When he lifted his head, she saw he was puzzled, a slight frown dented his brow.

"What's wrong?" he asked, his voice still slurred with passion.

"I was wondering how long it would take me to pack."

He was frozen for a fraction of time. "Don't say such foolish things."

"It's not foolish. I can't stay."

"Why not?" She didn't answer and he pressed his palms into her cheeks. "Why not?" he demanded hoarsely.

Julie shook her head helplessly. What could she possibly say? She couldn't tell him the truth and she couldn't bring herself to lie to him.

"Tell me what's wrong. I'm not letting you leave until you tell me," he said unsteadily.

Knowing he meant what he said, she gave in and explained, "I can't be your live-in lover while you dance around town with women like your Serena Seifert."

Cameron almost fainted with relief. Jealous! She was simply jealous! He moved his hands to tenderly stroke her hair. "Dearest, I've found dancing with more than one partner at a time tends to bruise the toes." She didn't even smile, so he skimmed a finger over her lips. "I won't do that to you, Julie, I swear it. While we're together, I'll be all yours. And of all the women in

Chicago to worry about, Serena should be the last on your list. Serena is my secretary."

He saw the knowing look Julie threw him and laughed. Thinking he was making light of her deepest emotions, Julie shut her eyes. She felt his lips brush her eyelids and promptly opened them again.

"People always think just what you're thinking, but it isn't true. I don't give a damn how alluring—"

So you admit she's alluring! her eyes accused.

"She may be," he continued firmly. "I hired her for two reasons. She can do her job, and she knows how to keep her mouth shut. Even if I had designs on her—which I do not—her husband could flatten me without having to take a breath. He was a linebacker for the Bears, and he's twice my size."

He didn't know if he'd convinced her. He wasn't going to waste time trying to find out. Instead, he began kissing her urgently, caressing her feverishly. When he felt her tremble, he slowed. He took the time to explore the special texture of her soft smooth skin. He savored the feel of her beneath his fingertips and the taste of her beneath his lips. Gradually he felt her responding to his lightest touch.

Julie couldn't maintain her defenses against this practiced assault. She didn't fully believe him about Serena, but she didn't want to disbelieve him either. So she shoved the problem aside and surrendered her senses to his control, shuddering and sighing at the command of his hands and lips.

This time Cam controlled his needs, making himself wait until he'd completely broken through her built-up reserve. He took her gently, changing rhythms and prolonging the pleasure until he thought he would die with the sweetness of it. At last he felt her body go taut within his arms. Only then did he let himself give in to the shattering of his own excitement.

He rolled onto his side, watching the flush fade from her cheeks. He kissed her jawline and stroked the soft down of her stomach. Finally her lashes fluttered and she looked at him. Her eyes were darkly blue, passion-filled, and sleepy. Gazing into them, he leaned forward.

"Stay with me, Julia," he whispered.

CHAPTER NINE

Julia stayed.

She'd lain within Cam's warm embrace and let her physical and mental exhaustion overcome her. When she awoke, she was alone. She stretched beneath a light blanket, feeling intensely, pleasurably sated. As her eyes adjusted to the darkened room she noticed that her suitcase and clothes were no longer strewn over the floor.

Had she dreamed it all? Not knowing whether she wanted to believe she'd actually made love to Cam, Julie rose and dressed quietly. She discovered her clothing back in her drawers and her suitcase back on the top shelf of the closet. Tucking her hair neatly into shape, she set out in search of Cam.

She found him in the kitchen, his shirt-sleeves rolled up as he washed a mound of glasses. She noted that the debris of the party had been cleared away, though stains on floor and counter remained as visible evidence of the night before. Standing on the tips of her feet, poised to slip away, she stood in the doorway and watched him work. He reached for a glass and she felt him reaching for her. Her nerves cartwheeled at the memory of his touch. Her body quivered, and Julie knew it had not been a dream.

Cam suddenly looked over his shoulder. For a moment he stared at her blankly. Then he smiled. It was a confident smile, but the glint in his eyes was wary, questioning.

"It's about time you woke up, lazybones," he said on a carefully casual note. "Do you realize it's nearly five?"

She stood looking at him mutely. It was the expressionless, emotionless Julia looking at him now and, watching her, frustration flooded Cam. He'd thought their mutual passion had destroyed these barriers. Now it appeared they were back where they'd started. He kept his smile in place, but an inch of ice caked it.

"You've timed it neatly, I must say," he went on conversationally. "You wait until I'm on the last of the washing up to appear. I've got a case of dishpan hands you wouldn't believe. First thing tomorrow, I'm going out to buy us a dishwasher."

A massive lump had settled in Julie's throat, making it impossible for her to speak. It was just as well, because she had no idea what to say. The only thing she wanted to say was the one thing she must never say to him. She could never openly reveal her love.

He pulled his hands from the sudsy water and began drying them on a towel. Irritation was rapidly mounting. She wasn't acting like a woman to whom he'd made passionate love. She should be dewy-eyed and softly smiling, not staring at him as if he'd just sprouted another head.

"Are you hungry?" he asked tersely.

Julie shook her head, her blond hair flying slightly. He tossed down the towel and took a step forward. She backed a step and he halted, his anger flaring. Damn her, damn her, damn her. He wanted to wring her neck, he wanted to shake her until her teeth rattled, he wanted to kiss her breathless.

"Julie, about last night," he said just as she exclaimed, "Cameron, I'm sorry!"

They broke off and stared at one another. Cam's brows snapped down. "Sorry? For what?"

She had meant to tell him *I'm sorry, but I must leave.* She gazed into the brown eyes steadily scowling at her and knew she couldn't go. Not yet. Later, later she would have the courage to leave, but not yet, she lied to herself. So she faced the frown he was fixing on her and said, "For letting you do all the cleaning up. You should have wakened me so I could help."

It was only as he released his breath that Cam realized he'd been holding it. Sensing she wasn't ready to be rushed, he suppressed his urge to sweep her into his arms and said as evenly as he could, "You needed the rest. And you need to eat. You haven't had anything since yesterday."

She let him fix her a simple meal, but only after she helped him finish the washing and drying. As they worked Cam talked about various people who'd been at the party, who they were, what they did, how he'd got to know them. Once his arm grazed hers, and she jumped, turning startled eyes upon him. Her skin jangled, and her nerves seemed to bounce like rubber. She throbbed beneath the dark intention in his eyes. Finally he turned back to wiping glasses, continuing his friendly monologue until Julie gradually calmed.

After they'd eaten, they spent the evening in the study with the television providing noise and action to cover the stillness between them. As she had before, Julie sat curled on the floor, leaning against the sofa. She was intensely aware of Cam sitting behind her, her blood pounding with each breath he took. Her eyes fixed on the changing colors on the screen and her mind fixed on the wild clattering of her heart.

What was going to happen? What if he asked her to sleep with him tonight? What if he didn't? Should she slip off to her room now or wait for him to say something? And what should she say if he did? What should she do if he did nothing? Oh, dear God, what should she do?

Cameron couldn't sit still. He suffered an unaccustomed agony of indecision. He stared at Julia sitting below him and ached to hold her. But he was afraid she didn't want him. Should he simply grab her and start kissing or wait for her to give him a sign? But what if she never gave him a sign? What if she got up and went to her room alone? What should he do?

He repositioned himself on the sofa and drummed his fingers on the arm. He gazed at the lamplight lacing into her hair and remembered the silken softness of it. It triggered a volley of arousing sensations. The warm pliancy of her breasts, the grainy texture of her taut nipples, the sweet scent of talc clinging to her skin. He felt himself stirring at the memories and knew he should stop the flow of thought. He shifted against the cord cushions and cleared his throat.

"What would you like to watch next?" he asked.

She turned her head and smiled. "Whatever you like." Looking back at the TV, Julie hoped he hadn't seen her pulse beating fiercely in her throat. The brief glimpse of him made her mouth go dry. His shirt was halfway unbuttoned. She'd seen the hint of his chest and remembered the firm warmth of it, the tousled downiness of hair there. She had wanted to remember every moment of making love to him, and now she did. She remembered—and she tingled with a rising need.

At the end of every program Cam inquired what she'd like to watch, and Julie answered, "Anything you like." Finally, after endless, meaningless shows, the ten o'clock news came on. Feeling a leaden disappointment, Julie decided she should go on into her bedroom. She gracefully came to her feet.

That same instant Cameron jumped up. They collided and before either could speak, they were tangled together, kissing and caressing in writhing hunger. Passion consumed them. Folding Julie into his arms, Cam carried her into his room, kicking the door closed behind him.

And so Julia stayed.

Humming cheerfully, Julie checked the contents of the wicker picnic basket. Ham-and-cheese sandwiches, a package of chips, sweet butter pickles in a jar, a ball of Gouda cheese, and a cellophane roll of crackers were jumbled in with a bottle of wine and two glasses. She shook her head, smiling at Cam's idea of the way to pack a basket, and rearranged the items into an orderly whole. The pickles had leaked slightly, so she transferred them to another jar with a tighter lid. She'd just finished when Cam threw his arms around her waist and nuzzled his lips into her nape.

"Ummm, you smell like pickle juice," he said as he whirled her around to plant a kiss on her nose.

"It's the latest in perfumes. Guaranteed to drive a man to the nearest picnic," she responded, laughing breathlessly. It seemed she was always out of breath when he was near. She kissed his chin, then his lips. "You pack a mighty poor picnic, Mr. Stone. Nary a napkin, and how were we supposed to open the wine without a corkscrew?"

"So who needs wine? You're heady enough for me," he murmured as he cupped her breasts with his palms.

She playfully slapped at his hands. "Don't be starting that—we'll never get to the concert if you do!"

"That's okay with me," he said with a wicked gleam in his eye. "We can make our own music. Play our love song."

"I think the orchestra will be more in tune." Julia twirled away from his arms. "We'll leave as soon as I get washed up."

The phone shrieked from her bedroom while she was scrubbing the acrid odor of pickles off her hands. It was her personal line, and unless she said something, Cam would ignore it. At the second shrill she called out, "Get that, will you Cam?" then quickly began rinsing soap from her fingers. She hurriedly toweled her hands and walked into her room in time to hear him say, "No, Mrs. Hollis."

Julie's heart sank to her toes. Her mother had no idea she was sharing her apartment with a man. Her appalled dismay stamped itself clearly on her face.

Seeing the pleading in Julie's widened eyes, Cam said swiftly, "No, ma'am, I'm the electrician. I'm installing a new line. Yes, ma'am. She's in the kitchen. I'll get her."

Gratitude fought with embarrassment to be uppermost in Julie's emotions as she took the receiver from his hand. Gratitude won, and she shot him a look of heartfelt thanks before speaking into the phone. Cam left the room, granting her privacy for the few minutes she conversed with her mother, but he pounced on her as soon as she hung up.

"What's up?" he asked in a deceptively casual way as she joined him at the front door.

Embarrassment now came to the fore. "Oh, nothing really. Mom says my father thinks it's time for me to make a trip home. I told her I'd come for a visit as soon as I could take my vacation." Julie paused. "She lectured me about having an electrician in on overtime hours."

Actually her mother had grilled her about the electrician's age—and whether or not he wore a ring on his left hand. Laura Hollis viewed her daughter's spinsterhood as a willful act of defiance designed to humiliate her among the members of her garden club, all of whom were now reporting on the progress of their grandchildren while Laura still reported on the progress of Julia's *career*. Julie knew precisely how her mother would have reacted to the news that Cam was her lover, and the thought made her shudder. She drew in her bottom lip. "Thanks for the quick thinking. It's ridiculous, isn't it? At my age to be afraid to tell my mother I'm living with a man?"

He handed her into his car and walked around to get in on his side before responding. "No, not ridiculous. Just a bit old-fashioned."

He didn't see her wince at the word. As they drove along, Julie told herself she would *not* think about her mother. She gazed fixedly at all the countless shades of green in the passing array of lushly verdant trees, shrubs, and grasses. Spring had been unusually wet—a thundering roll of stormy skies, windy days, and chilled nights. But the continual rains had cleansed the city until even the dirt of Chicago seemed scrubbed, and the June air smelled fresh. Peering through the leafy patchwork of a tree, Julie eyed the graying sky with a worried frown.

"Do you think it will rain?" she asked Cam as they idled at a stoplight.

He caressed her with a sensual smile. "If it does, we'll come back and picnic in private."

She raised her brow at him, but sank back into the leather seat feeling content, her mother forgotten in the aura of Cam's smile. Was it possible to be this happy? she asked herself. As the breeze through the open window whisked through her hair, Julie shut her eyes and mused about all the teasing warmth they'd shared through the love-tossed nights of the stormy spring.

She thought about Easter, when Cam had hidden plastic eggs throughout the apartment and directed her on a hunt. Inside each was a note telling her where to look for the next. The last egg directed her to his bedroom—their bedroom, now, she corrected herself—where she'd found a gigantic basket filled with chocolates. And behind the basket Cam had been waiting with a grin. They'd romped gleefully through chocolates and into playful loving.

She thought about the party he'd taken her to on May Day, where he'd introduced her to Joe Seifert, Serena's husband. Joe had grinned, displaying brawn even in his smile, and boomed hello. Dwarfed beside the beefy Joe, Cam had held her gaze, as if to say *See? I'd have to have a death wish to fool with this man's wife!* And much later, when they'd come home, Cam had undressed her slowly, cataloguing each feature of her body that outshone every other woman he'd seen at the party, including the voluptuous Serena. Their lovemaking that night had been a slow-moving, tender waltz.

She thought about the night she'd slipped on the rickety basement steps at work. At M.B.'s call Cam had rushed to the shop. When he realized Julie's only injuries were a twisted ankle and a bruised behind, his frantic worry had turned to anger at her carelessness. He'd lectured her all the way home and had practically flung her into bed upon arrival. He'd loved her so furiously, a spring broke in the bed and it now creaked whenever they made love. Cam called it their love song. . . .

Love. Inwardly Julie sighed. It was the only blot on her happiness. She strove hard to ignore it, but there were constant, unexpected moments like now, when a splinter of discontent pricked at her. She peeked at Cam's profile through the curtain of her lowered lashes. He cared, she knew he did. He told her often and with great feeling that he loved her. Why couldn't she be satisfied with that?

Because she didn't trust his words of love. Allen, too, had said he loved her. Words were too easily spoken, Julia mused—and too easily forgotten. When Cam whispered his love against her naked body, the dagger of doubt would strike, and she would wonder how long she had until he tired of loving her. Julie wanted the one thing Cam apparently couldn't give: She wanted him to sheath that dagger, to commit his love to her, permanently.

He was loving—he was even faithful. He'd said to her, "While we're together, I'll be all yours," and he'd kept his word. But the hidden threat in that statement haunted Julia. The echo of *while we're together* was the shadow encroaching on her brightness. Whenever she felt tempted to tell Cam of her love, she heard the echo, saw the shadow, and remained silent.

One teasing smile, one flick of his fingertip against her cheek—that was all it took to chase away the dull grayness. But it always crept back. Like now.

As if he sensed the sudden downshift in her mood, Cam turned his head and delivered just that type of smile. The heart-stopping kind that left Julie feeling dizzy. She returned his smile and shoved the clouds out of her skies, determined to enjoy every moment she had with him, while she had them to enjoy.

Cam easily parked the Jag in a tight spot on Columbus Drive a few blocks from Grant Park. They joined the steady stream of people flowing toward the band shell behind the Art Institute. Nearing the edifice of the Institute, they exchanged an intimate smile of reminiscence, then consciously focused on the scene taking shape on the grassy expanse before them. This was the sort of event that brought the colorful variety of Chicago to the fore. A free symphony in the park, enjoyed equally by young and old.

Holding tightly to Cam's hand, Julie felt her spirits lift as she took in the festive mood. Women passed by in flowing prairie skirts, tight shorts, baggy jeans. Men in suits, in jeans, even in tuxedos, followed them. Toddlers wobbled by on short chubby legs, chased by harried parents. People toted picnic hampers, baby strollers, dogs on leashes. A kilted Scotsman carried a bagpipe. In the same instant Julie and Cam looked at each other and laughed out loud.

They ignored the seats positioned before the band shell and spread out their red plaid stadium blanket on an unclaimed spot of grass. They settled down to eat their picnic amid hundreds of others doing the same. Some set up aluminum lounges; some were sprawled on the grass. Not far from where they sat a young couple had improvised a small table out of a box and decorated it with a candle in a bottle and a red rose.

"Look at that," said Cam, pointing with his ham-and-cheese sandwich.

"What?" Julie saw several young men flipping Frisbees between the trees and an energetic girl scaling the branches of one.

"That guy over there with the Walkman. Can you imagine going to an outdoor concert and shutting the sound out with headphones?" Cam chuckled and shook his head. "People. They never cease to amaze me." She laughed her sparkling laugh, and his eyes softened. "Especially you," he added in a tone that took her breath away.

"Me?" she squeaked. "How could I amaze you? You know practically everything there is to know about Julia Jean Hollis—and then some."

"It's the *then some* part that I like best," drawled Cam suggestively. He looked around at the ever-changing sea of people and eventually brought his gaze back to her long thin lovely face. "You're like all these people rolled into one, Julia, and I never know which one is going to appear next. One day you're like that grandmother who's so serenely knitting over there. The next you're like that tomboy climbing the tree. I never know just what to expect from you."

"Don't you think we're all like that? That we're all a combination of people coming together to form one unique person?" She gazed at him with her nose crinkled, and her eyes narrowed intently. "You, for example. Sometimes you're as boyish as those kids throwing Frisbees. Other times you're like that romantic behind us who just kissed his girl over the candlelight."

"Oh? Did he singe his chin?" he teased.

She shook her head, strands of blond flaring outward. "And most times you're just plain ornery. Who'd have expected the great rock 'n' roll fan to bring me to a symphony concert?"

They laughed, then ate while enjoying the music that meandered through the trees. The sky faded from blue-gray to a subdued pink as night leisurely crept in over the crowd. Evening lights struck one by one against the invading darkness. People danced, talked, laughed. Planes droned in the distance overhead, and police helicopters occasionally buzzed by. Julie nestled into Cam's embrace, listening dreamily to Tchaikovsky and Dvořak.

At the intermission they were about to pour the last of their Chablis when a honeyed voice poured over them. "Cam! I *thought* it must be you, but I couldn't be absolutely certain! You've kept yourself so hidden the last few months. . . ."

The feminine tones had risen and fallen alternately with each word, ending on a low note parroted by the plummeting of Julie's heart. The woman slipped into place beside Cam with an ease that made it appear it was the most natural place for her to be. She was small and curvy, with full breasts and hips that Julie immediately hoped would turn to fat by middle age. Her hair matched her voice: a honey-brown that flowed past her shoulders. Julie watched Cam's lips curve sensually at the woman and felt all her enjoyment in the evening evaporate.

"Hi, Barb," he said easily. "What've you been up to?"

"Nothing special, same old rounds. How did you manage to get off the carousel?" she asked, shooting a coy look at Julia. Gritting her teeth, Julie managed a thin smile.

"Oh. Barb Lindelof, I'd like you to meet Julia Hollis."

" 'Lo," said Barb with the briefest of nods to Julie. "By the way, Dennis said to send you over, Cam. He's got some beer and a couple of questions about that Wrigley Field gig for Whiplash. Dennis is their agent, you know," she said in a condescending aside to Julie as she pointed out the general direction of Dennis's whereabouts to Cam.

Telling Julie he'd be right back, Cam sprang up and off. Julie felt annoyed. First because he didn't think to take her to meet his friend, and second because he left her with a woman she was certain she didn't want to like. She wondered why Barb stayed. She soon learned why. Barb wanted her curiosity salved.

"So you're Cameron's mysterious lady," she said on a lengthy drawl. The pitch of the last word dipped, making it sound like an accusation. "Cam used to be the life of every party, but nobody sees him anymore. We've been wondering if you keep him under lock and key." She paused, looking Julie up and down. Julie fought to keep her smile from slipping off her face.

Barb swiveled her head around, then sighed. "I do love these Grant Park concerts. They're *so* romantic." Another sigh, deep and flowing. "I remember when Cam brought me here last summer—"

"Cam was here with you?" The instant Julie said it, she wished she hadn't. But she hadn't been able to help herself.

"Oh, yes. We were what you could call an item in those days," confided Barb with a sultry laugh. She tapped her hand on Julia's knee. "That was before I met Dennis, of course."

The flash of a diamond ring streaked through the darkening night. "Of course," agreed Julie in a dead voice.

"Well, I must get back. *Do* make Cam bring you over sometime. All his friends are wondering why we never see him."

She was gone, leaving behind a cloying scent of heavy perfume and a totally dejected Julia. All her worst fears had been embodied in that brief exchange. By this time next year would Cam be sitting here with his arms wrapped around another woman? Would she be looking back and speaking of their relationship in the past tense? Had Barb realized he wouldn't make a commitment and gone looking for someone who would? Or had Cam decided it was time to move on to someone new?

The questions badgered her endlessly throughout the intermission. The meeting with Barb Lindelof magnified the vague disquiet she'd felt since talking to her mother earlier. By the time the orchestra reappeared on the band shell, Cam still hadn't returned and Julie's depression began to harden. She drew up her knees, hugging them against her chest while resting her chin on them as if her head had grown too heavy to hold up. Not really listening to the selection from Rimski-Korsakov's *Le Coq d'or,* she waged a mental debate with herself.

She was being ridiculous. Cam loved her. He told her he did; he showed her in a thousand little ways that he did. If he didn't show her in the one way she needed, did it really matter? Love didn't require marriage to last, did it? And so what if it didn't last forever. She should enjoy it while it did last. Why ruin what she had by being depressed now? She should wait until he was gone to feel miserable.

But Julie felt miserable now. It was a dead-end relationship, she thought, and she was running out of roadway. How much longer? Julie asked herself. How much longer until he told her it wasn't fun anymore, until he told her it was over?

Cam slid onto the blanket beside her, facing her. She didn't move, remaining stiffly coiled. Imitating her, he drew up his knees. "Sorry I was gone so long, but I was talking business."

She was afraid that if she opened her mouth to speak, a wail of woe would tumble out, so she said nothing. She cast one quick sidelong look at him, then hastily looked down at her toes. It didn't seem to matter that she'd been unable to see much of his shadowed face. Just the mere fact that he was *there,* a hair-breadth away, raised bumps on her skin.

He waited several minutes before bringing the back of his hand up to brush gently over her cheek. He heard her sharply drawn breath and inquired softly, "What's wrong, sweetheart? I really am sorry I left you alone so long."

"It doesn't matter."

Her flat tones told him it did. He dropped his hand to her shoulder, tracing a pattern up and down her arm with his fingers. She remained so cold, he felt as if the tips of his fingers were being frostbitten. "Do you want to talk? Or just listen to the music?"

"Music," she answered through tight lips. She wanted to shout *Just leave me and get it over with! Put me out of my misery!* But she stared straight ahead, saying nothing at all.

Cameron was tempted to ask her again to tell him whatever was troubling her, but her expression wasn't encouraging. He removed his hand from her arm and sat silently, watching her for the remainder of the concert. While all around them people were standing and dancing, yelling for more, they were immobile, two statues bitterly aware of nothing beyond each other.

Wordlessly they stood and gathered their things together. Cam noticed how Julie inched away from him, avoiding the least contact. Uncertain what to say, he said nothing. When they were settled into the car, ready to leave, he glanced at her profile and suddenly turned off the ignition.

"About Dennis—"

"What are we waiting here for?" she interrupted coldly.

He stared a moment at the remote stillness of her pale face, then abruptly switched the ignition back on. The Jag shot out of the parking space with a roar that sent Julie's stomach lurching upward. His jaw was set, his lips thinned as he wove the car wildly through the thick traffic. She wanted to beg him to stop taking such crazy chances, but recognizing that this was precisely what he wanted, she squeezed her eyes shut and swallowed her protests.

Somehow they arrived home intact. Julie jumped out of the car and dashed into the apartment. There she sank into one of the wingback chairs. She was still visibly shaking when Cam entered, carrying both the blanket and the basket. She picked up the first magazine her hand met and thrust her nose into a six-month-old issue of *NFL Illustrated.* She didn't look up, but she was terribly aware of the belligerent manner in which he dropped the picnic gear, of the way he stalked to stand in front of the chair. She remained immersed in her magazine.

"Developing a new interest in football?" asked Cam.

"Umm," she replied.

In one swift jerk he yanked the magazine from her hands. Her mouth opened, but the taut determination in his face left her incapable of uttering an objection. Tossing the magazine into the air, Cam reached for her and she flailed her hands in weak defense. He clasped them and pulled her up as easily as he had taken the magazine. He drew her against his chest. She could feel the slow thud of his heart beneath her palms.

"Julie, whatever's wrong, remember this," he said in measured deliberation. "I love you."

"Don't tell me—show me!" she burst out, wishing he'd prove his feelings for her with a commitment of his heart. But Cam took her literally. With an unsteady breath he tilted her head back and slowly lowered his lips to meet hers.

It was a worshipful kiss—as if she were sacred, wondrous, prized above all else. It was a kiss to heal Julia's wounded pride, to still her tumultuous fears. Her resistance to him crumbled in the hushed urgency of that kiss.

Feeling the change in her, Cam swirled his hands restlessly along her spine, then swept them up her sides to the uplift of her breasts. Her nipples hardened to the command of his caressing thumbs, and Julie arched toward him, wanting to be closer, to be part of him.

They reluctantly broke apart, gazing hungrily for a beat of time. Each saw passion reflected in the other's eyes. Linking hands, they stumbled into the bedroom. Silently, almost solemnly, they undressed and drifted back into each other's arms. Clinging together, they tumbled onto the bed. It squeaked loudly in protest, transforming the mystical mood into merriment. Their laughter was muffled in the meeting of their lips.

Cameron folded his body over Julia's and pressed her back into the creaking mattress. "Love song," murmured Cam at the edge of her mouth. "Play it for me, Julie."

She twined her fingers in his hair and pulled his mouth down to cover hers. As she tantalized his lips with her tongue she teased his flesh with her touch, kneading the sinews of his shoulders with her cool fingers. She felt him tense, heard his breath come in deep rasps, and knew an exhilaration. No matter what might come later, for this moment he was hers, all hers.

Sliding his hands to her hips, Cam shifted himself above her. As he entered her body he sighed into the curve of her throat, "Do you know what you do to me, dearest? Do you know"—he nibbled lightly up to her chin—"how you make me feel?"

Swaying to the pillowy cadence of their love, Julie curled her fingers into the muscles of his back and gasped, "No. Tell me, tell me."

"Like . . . I'm bound to you," he said in a voice thick with passion. "Bondage—without the ropes. . . ."

With a deep gutteral groan Cam thrust forward. The bed began singing, and Julie's doubts were muted in the crescendo.

CHAPTER TEN

Two raindrops hit the window and merged together, coursing downward as one. Julia focused on the drops and thought of Cameron coming to her, merging with her. A warmth stole over her, and she strove to peer beyond the misted window of the taxi into the veil of steady rain. A blurry torrent of cars rushed by, all intent on getting beyond the flood of traffic snarling O'Hare Airport. Gradually her eyes wandered back to where the rivulet had been and she smiled.

Would Cam be as eager to touch and taste and come together as she? She'd only been gone a week, but to Julie it felt like a lifetime. She hoped it felt that way to him, too, and she daydreamed about Cam's look of surprise when she walked in. Her original flight was scheduled to arrive later that night, but she'd been too impatient, too eager to be with him again. Early this morning, her parents had driven her to Huron, the nearest city to her hometown serviced by an airport, where Julie had caught an earlier flight out. She thought again of Cam's surprise and suppressed the urge to demand the cabbie step on it.

Perhaps, she reflected as she settled back into the corner of the cab, the separation had been beneficial. The days apart had settled things in her own mind at least. She was now absolutely certain that she wanted nothing more in life than to be with Cam. As much as she'd wanted to visit her parents, Julie had spent the week impatient to get home, to be with him. Their brief long-distance calls had only tantalized her, filling her with the need to be together.

Since the night of the concert back in June, they'd been together almost constantly. Cam seemed reluctant to leave her alone, and Julie had basked in his attention, occasionally even daring to feel secure about their relationship. They didn't need a piece of paper to secure their love, she would tell herself firmly whenever doubt attempted to intrude on her happiness.

Her mother, of course, held a completely different view. It was her opinion that if Julia had a man interested enough to call her every night from Chicago, he should be interested enough to marry her. But whenever Laura Hollis had an opinion she knew would be received unpleasantly, she expressed it obliquely, presenting it as Art's belief. This time had been no exception.

"How happy we were to hear your friends' good news," her mother had said with the slightest of accusing looks at her. "You must tell Mary Beth and Gregory that we'd be thrilled to act as surrogate grandparents any time. Your father was saying just the other day that he'd be even more thrilled to be a *real* grandfather. But of course, I promptly reminded him that you're still not married."

Julie watched her mother sweep a hand through her short, silvered blond hair and murmured, "Yes, I'm not."

As Laura's voice droned onward in expression of Art Hollis's opinions on Julia's life-style, her daughter drifted away to a memory of laughter.

Fireworks hadn't been any more dazzling than Mary Beth Farrow on the Fourth of July. Her dark eyes were sparkling, and even her freckles seemed to glitter as she broke the news over lemonade and chocolate-chip cookies. It was, she stated emphatically, Cam and Julie's fault.

"Our fault!" they chorused while staring dumbfounded at a beaming Greg.

"Yes, *yours,*" repeated M.B., wagging an accusing finger at the pair of them. "It was the night of your party back at the end of

March. We went home a little—Well, let's just say we weren't in any condition to remember precautions. And *voilà*!"

The four had laughed and toasted the baby. Cam added a toast to the party itself, then shot a hot look brimming with meaning at a flushing Julie as Greg and M.B. exchanged puzzled glances. Thinking of it now, she felt another light heat rush over her. Looking up, she saw her mother frowning at her and tried hard to pay attention.

"Your father wondered what it is that this Cameron does for a living?" Laura busied herself with checking the bread baking in the oven, not meeting Julia's amused gaze.

She fielded such queries all week long, sometimes with humor, sometimes with exasperation, always with loving insight. She understood that her mother was saying *So why aren't you married to this man you love, who seems to love you, and giving me some grandchildren?* Knowing she had no real answer to this, afraid to question Cam's refusal to make the ultimate commitment to her, she endured the probing and dodged the questions as best she could.

The cab was nearing the apartment. Julie inched forward on the edge of the seat and swiped impatiently at the window with the back of her hand. The rain was tapering off to a light drizzle, and she could clearly see the trees shaking droplets from their leaves onto darkly dampened pavements. As the familiar landscape of her neighborhood neared, her every nerve end rippled with anticipation. Soon, soon, she would see Cam!

She saw him sooner than she expected. As the cab drew into her block, the door of their building opened and Cam strode out. Her heart swung up, then dived down as she noticed the suitcase in his hand.

"Wait a minute," she said, tapping the driver on the shoulder. "Stop here, please."

"Whatever you say, lady," said the cabbie with a shrug. He obediently pulled to the curb and waited.

Cam held the apartment door wide and a moment later a

young woman walked out. She was tall and tan, and to Julia's eyes she might as well have been naked. Her bright yellow tube top hugged her generous breasts precariously, and her shorts scarcely covered her perky bottom. The smile she tossed at Cam was teasing—and intimate. They rounded the corner of the building, walking toward the carports. Julia sat frozen, immobile. A few minutes later, Cam's Jag tore out of the lot, complete with passenger. His car disappeared from view, and still, Julia sat, unable to move.

This can't be happening! she told herself. Yet, even as she denied what she'd seen, Julia's disbelief was transformed into acceptance. A bitterly sharp, stabbing acceptance. She'd expected this from the beginning. It was what she'd known would happen. She'd known, too, that it would hurt, but not like this! Not this agonizing rending of her soul.

"You wanna sit here all day, lady?" asked the cabbie, looking at her through his mirror.

Her eyes blankly met his. She shook her head, then said in a voice that cracked, "No. Take me back to O'Hare. Now, please."

"O'Hare?" His heavy jowls shifted as he put his lips together in a silent whistle. She saw his understanding and looked away. She couldn't bear having a witness to her heartbreak. "Okay, lady," he acceded as he steered his cab into a U-turn.

All those nights when she'd lain alone in her bed in South Dakota, yearning for the feel of Cam beside her, he'd obviously been longing for nothing. He'd filled the empty place in his bed. How could he do that? How could he whisper words of love to her over the phone while enacting them with someone else? Julia felt sick, physically sick. She'd given Cam something far more precious than her body, even more fragile than her love: She'd given him her trust, and he'd betrayed her.

What could she do? The thought of returning to the apartment —to sleep where that girl had slept—disgusted her. And yet, not to return, not to have Cam's arms around her at night, was unthinkable. He'd made himself necessary to her, damn him! By the time the taxi pulled into the departures stand at O'Hare, Julie had no notion why she'd told the driver to take her to the airport. But she paid him, thanked him, and moved to join the conflux of people flowing into the busy airport terminal.

"Hey, lady," called the cabbie before she walked away. She turned and stared unseeing into his kind eyes. "Take my advice. Forget him."

She watched him drive away and wondered how she kept from crying. Forget Cam, Julie told herself. As if she could.

She'd thought she knew Cameron Stone. Obviously she didn't. He was a stranger to her. She'd given him so much, she could only be thankful she'd never let him know she'd also given him her heart. Though she'd revealed in countless ways with her eyes, her hands, her lips, she'd never once told Cam how she felt. At first she'd feared how much more hurt she'd be when he left. Lately she'd feared facing the enormity of her increasing love. Now that protective instinct would at least enable her to salvage her pride.

A small child bumped into her, knocking her suitcase against her knee. Julia started and looked around, as if just now realizing where she was. She checked her watch. It was five hours until her original flight was due in. Walking with the precise steps of an automaton, she found a locker, stored her bag, then retreated to a dimly lighted seat in one of the bars. She ordered a ginger ale, then sat in a personal vacuum untouched by the continual hum of activity surrounding her. The fluctuating tides of people passed by unnoticed. She stared at her hands folded in the lap of her orchid-print sundress. Her dress was new; she had worn it to surprise Cam, who so often told her she dressed too plainly. Perhaps, she now mused, she should have worn a tube top and nearly non-existent shorts.

Over the next four hours Julie tortured herself by painfully examining every splinter of her heartbreak. She reviewed her relationship with Cam from the day they'd met, almost delighting in the piercing pain her memories delivered. She pictured him in the mornings, his hair rumpled over the pillow, his jaw rough with stubble, and his eyes filled with sleepy desire. Or at night with shadows casting his face into dark relief and his hands showing her his need.

Angrily Julie thrust the images from her mind. But with tormenting tenacity they always returned. At last she paid for her succession of unwanted ginger ales and left the bar. After retrieving her suitcase, she went to the concourse gate where her original flight was due to arrive. All those hours of thinking and she still hadn't sorted out what she intended to do. Her impulse to catch the first flight out had been discarded as soon as she entered the airport. She couldn't run away, not without speaking to Cam. But she had no idea what she should say to him.

She stood looking out the plate-glass window. The gray sky hung low, oppressively heavy: a precise complement to the way she felt.

A pair of hands slid around her waist, a pair of lips nuzzled the sensitive shell of her ear. "I vant to kiss zee inside uff your thigh," announced Cam on a wicked whisper.

The warmth of his arms seared through Julie's sundress into her skin. Even if he hadn't spoken, she'd have known him by his touch. At the graze of his lips her heart had fiercely slammed against her ribs. At the soughing of his voice her breathing apparatus had skidded to a stop. Self-anger swelled within her. She resented the reaction of her body to the mere presence of him. Had she no pride? He'd just come from another woman! Had he kissed the inside of *her* thigh?

Her resentful thoughts whirled in the brief seconds that Cam placed a kiss beside his whisper and spun her around. He was grinning, his face filled with blatant pleasure. "Julie, Julie, what are you doing here? Your plane's not due to arrive for another forty minutes."

Her eyes slued past him, anxious to view anything else but the disturbing excitement in his gaze. In that brief glimpse she noted that he'd changed since this afternoon. He now wore a lemon polo shirt with short sleeves and perfectly pressed tan slacks. His hands moved to her shoulders, and she focused on the hair dusting his forearms. She answered with a flat "I came in on an earlier flight."

Cameron ran his hands lightly over her bare shoulders. She'd got some sun while she was gone, and the faint glaze of bronze accentuated the blond of her hair, the blue of her eyes. He wondered just where her tan ended and felt his need for her stir within him.

"Why didn't you call me? I'd have come right out. God, how I've wanted to be with you!"

Despite the muggy summer heat Julia felt cold, ice-cold. A shiver began at the curve of her shoulders and quivered downward, forming icicles to her very core. From within her frozen depths she summoned up a chill voice. "Oh? You were home?"

Hearing the monotone of her reply, Cam felt dread seeping into his veins. He gazed at her expressionless face and slowly lowered his hands. He'd arrived early, eager to see her, to hold her. When he'd unexpectedly found her already there, his adrenaline had spurted into full-time production. Now he stared at her, and his happiness withered.

"Of course," he answered. In cautiously neutral tones he probed, "Everything go okay with your folks?"

Julie felt none of the joy in this reunion she'd been anticipating all week. She didn't even feel the hostility and hurt she'd been experiencing all afternoon. Her emotions were drained. She felt nothing. Her emptiness was fully reflected in her empty tones. "Yes. It was a fine visit."

Irritation lanced at Cam. This wasn't going as he'd expected. All week he'd hungered to be with her again, to kiss her and caress her. He'd visualized her greeting him with laughter and breathless kisses, not this cool impassivity. What the hell was wrong? Why was she behaving like some stranger he'd politely agreed to meet?

"Do you want to stop for a drink in the bar before leaving?" he inquired on a snap.

She shook her head and bent to pick up her luggage. Cam reached the handle before her. Their fingers touched, and Julie jerked back as if stung. He scowled at her. "I'm not poisonous," he barked and strode down the concourse without looking to see if she followed.

Julie's electrified nerves jolted her down to her toes. How could she react so violently to such a brief glancing touch? She could because she loved him, she needed him. Trembling, she forced herself to follow Cameron briskly. Maybe, just maybe, if she tried hard enough, she could just forget what she'd seen this afternoon. She could pretend it never happened. She could pretend things were precisely the same as they'd been one week ago.

But Julia knew they weren't. And she didn't have the imagination necessary to make believe they were.

They strode out of the terminal into the multilevel parking lot. Their only exchanges were short polite phrases: *This way* from Cam or *Thank you* from Julie as he held open a door. They might indeed have been strangers meeting for the first time and not lovers who'd shared the most intimate of moments.

When Cam put her suitcase in the back of his Jag, Julie tried not to think about the other luggage that had been there earlier. When she sat in the seat, she tried not to think about the young woman who'd sat there. She tried not to think of the laughter she'd seen Cam sharing with that pretty girl as opposed to the leaden silence that now weighted between them.

Cam concentrated on getting out of the traffic of O'Hare before glancing at her rigid profile. The high swell of her breasts was emphasized by the tight bodice of her dress. He looked back at the road, feeling irritated. "That's a pretty dress," he said, sounding annoyed about it.

"Thank you," she returned with the enthusiasm of a robot.

The remainder of the drive was made in wordless animosity. At least, thought Cam, *he* felt angry. He doubted Julia felt anything. She was about as emotive as a zombie. He hadn't seen this Julia for months, and he didn't like seeing it now. Her reserve had always annoyed him far more than any of her outbursts. He didn't like thinking he couldn't get through to her. What had happened while she was gone? And what was he to do about it?

Julie stared fixedly out the car window, not seeing a thing. The rain had finally stopped; the storm vapors were clearing. The late summer sun strove to burst free of the lingering clouds, tinting the sky with occasional streaks of pinks and purples. She didn't give any of it so much as a glance. All she could focus on was the ache she felt within. Being near him, feeling the heat radiate from his skin, inhaling the maleness of him, was hammering a stake through her.

At the apartment Cam noted how carefully she avoided any contact with him, and he set his jaw to keep from shouting at her. As soon as he'd placed her suitcase on the bed, however, he stormed back out to the living room and demanded, "Okay, I've had enough of this, Julia. What's wrong? What happened? Did you have a fight with your parents, or have I done something?"

She'd been standing by the niche, staring out the windows, and wondering if Ms. Tube Top had curled up on the sofa as she liked to do. She slowly turned and looked at a point just beyond Cam's shoulder. "No."

A dark flush suffused his cheeks. "All right," he bit out as he moved toward her. "If you don't want to tell me—"

"Who was she?" interrupted Julie quietly.

"What?" Cam stopped in midstride to stare blankly at her. "Who was who?"

"Who was the girl you had staying here?"

She'd put the question in a totally dead voice, revealing none of the screeching pain she felt. She allowed herself a quick glance at Cam. His anger and puzzlement were dropping away. She couldn't quite believe it when he actually smiled.

"How did you . . .?" he began, then paused. "Is that what this is all about? Are you jealous?"

Before she could respond, Cam had crossed to her and pulled her into his arms. "You nearly gave me heart failure! I thought—Oh, hell, I thought you'd decided you didn't want to be coming back to me." He put her from him, tipped her head back, and met her tormented gaze directly, sincerely.

"Julie, she's my cousin! Patsy'd had a fight with her folks, and she ran away from home. She hopped on the nearest bus and ended up in Chicago without a dime. I let her stay here—in your old room—and tried to work out her problems with her parents. She went back home today. That's it. I can't believe you seriously thought there could have been anything else."

Julie stared into his dark eyes, searching desperately for the truth. She had to have time to sort it out, to sift through his words. But Cam gave her no time. He folded her within his firm arms and lowered his lips to hers. She fought to remain impassive, but her body defeated her. She gradually responded to the warmth of his kiss like an icicle melting in the sun. As she thawed, her arms came up to wreath his neck and he squeezed her so tight, she gasped for breath.

He released her, but only to draw her to the sofa. Keeping her hands clutched in his, he forced her to look at him. The thought of losing Julie had shaken him to the core. He'd never lacked masculine assurance in dealing with women. Until Julia. From the first he'd been unable to be certain about her, about what she thought and felt. He never really knew whether or not she wanted to stay with him. He still felt half alarmed, half angry with her. When he spoke, his voice was rough. "Tell me how you knew she was here."

"I wanted to—surprise you by arriving early. As the cab got here I saw you leaving with—her—with her suitcase. . . ." She looked away, embarrassed. She didn't want to give away too much, but she couldn't think of a convenient lie. All she could think of was the way her palms were tingling where his thumbs circled over the soft centers. She covered her nervousness with a shrug. "It looked pretty obvious, so I took the cab back to the airport."

"How could my practical Julia be so incredibly silly?" Softness stole into his voice, feathering her with the love of it. "You never thought of getting out of that cab and asking me what was going on? I'd have introduced you to Patsy."

She wanted to believe him, she *needed* to believe him. She bent her head. "I—I didn't think. I just saw and reacted."

Her words came out so hushed, Cam had to strain to hear them. An excitement pulsed in his veins at what he heard. For a very long time now, his prime desire had been to hear her say she cared. He sketched the outline of her lip with his fingertip, smiling as her mouth quivered. "What does all this mean, hmmm? Does all this jealousy mean you love me?"

She sat very still, refusing to face him, afraid that all her emotions would be revealed if she did. He chuckled quietly, sending hot breath over her cheek. "My God, how I've missed you," he whispered, bending toward her ear. His tongue flicked her lobe. "Did you miss me, my golden Julia?"

"Yes," she replied in a husky voice.

"How much?" he asked. He ringed her neck with his hands, stroking her jawline with his thumbs. He ached to hear her say she loved him, perhaps even more than he ached to taste again the sweetness of her love. He could feel her pulse beat rapidly against his palm and felt his own pound in fierce response.

She raised her lashes and was lost in the searing desire she saw in Cam's eyes. "This much," she murmured.

He shuddered as she pressed her fingers into the soft thickness of his hair and consumed him with a kiss. Her touch had the swirling, teasing lightness of dancing dust motes; her kiss had the heated richness of liquid gold. Moaning, he pushed her back into the mold of the sofa cushions. He buried his face against the hollow of her bare shoulder, tasting the powdery scent of her skin. In a muffled voice, he told her how he'd dreamed of this each night.

So have I, my darling, Julie responded in her mind. But she held back from putting it into words. More than ever she feared the power it would give him to shatter her soul. Instead, she whispered his name again and again, harmonizing with the melody of his musical kisses.

The thin straps of her sundress slipped from her shoulders and Cam gently slid his hands behind her. He fumbled for the zipper; Julie arched toward him and he tugged the metal downward. Somewhere deep, deep within Julie, a voice cried out to stop. She should push him away, get up and leave. She knew she was merely postponing the inevitable and magnifying her own heartache to come. But she didn't care. She didn't care for anything but feeding her hunger for this man. As he pushed her dress down, baring her breasts, she lifted up his shirt, baring his chest. Their flesh blazed at contact. They touched one another with predatory fervor.

Cameron kissed each peach tip of her breast, then lifted his head to gaze at her. Julia looked at him through a veil of lowered lashes and caught her breath at the sheer beauty of him. Moonlight sneaked from behind, gathering clouds to pour through the leaves of plants hanging in the windows. Glints of silver shimmered in his brown hair, and his eyes reflected pinpoints of moonglow; his lips curved sensually into the night shadows.

"How could you think," he asked in a husky voice, "that I would want anyone but you?"

The tips of her lashes lay upon her cheek. She saw an image of youthful legs and warm, full breasts. "I—I don't know. She was . . . so young and pretty."

The soft breath of his laughter caressed her. "Much too young. She tries to look older, but she's not a day over sixteen. Julie, Julie—how could you think I'd go after a kid like that? I'm not that hard up!" He paused, then laughed again. He drawled suggestively, "Well, maybe I am *now*. . . ."

She met his kiss with a bubble of joyful laughter, then she began feverishly exploring all the places she knew would most excite him. She didn't want any more talk. She wanted to still her nagging doubts as they had so often before—with wildly passionate love. Seeking desperately to be reassured, to be satisfied, Julia came to Cameron aggressively. Her ardor as they made love rocked them both.

In the flood of their passion the flames of her doubts were once again banked.

But not doused.

CHAPTER ELEVEN

Wailing winds rattled the windowpanes as they lay entwined. Cameron was the first to move. He stirred against Julia's warm body, then lifted his head.

"Sounds like the storm has returned."

"Mmmm," she agreed absently. Her fingers rhythmically stroked the sweat from his back. She felt him shiver at her touch.

"Don't you think"—he kissed her throat—"we should"—he kissed her jaw—"eat some dinner?" He kissed her lips, lightly, teasingly.

"Mmmm," repeated Julie. She kept her eyes closed, wanting this dream moment to go on and on and on.

"Is that a yes-mmm, a no-mmm, or a whatever-you-think-mmm?"

She lazily lifted her eyelids and caught the full force of his lopsided grin. She stretched beneath him, reveling in the feel of his hot skin rubbing against hers. "A whatever-you-think-mmm," she replied, blowing each word softly into his throat.

"I think, my dear, delightful one, that if you do that again, we won't be leaving this sofa for several hours to come."

His voice rasped, and his hands stressed his meaning with quick, hungry strokes up her ribcage. With a drawn-out sigh, Cam dropped a last kiss on the tip of her nose and slid from her embrace. He grasped her hands and pulled her to her feet. "Up with your lazy body—and what a body it is, I might add." He leered playfully as Julie blushed lightly.

He twirled her toward their bedroom, smartly patted her bare behind, and gently shoved. "Go unpack, and I'll throw together some eats. You can't ask for a fairer deal."

She heard his soft "I love you" as she skimmed in the direction he'd pointed her. She didn't acknowledge or answer, wishing he hadn't spoken. His words cut sharply into her dream. But when she was safely behind the closed bedroom door, Julie breathed a response to the air: "I love you, Cam."

She looked toward their bed. It was thoroughly rumpled, with one pillow hanging over the edge, the other balled against the headboard, and blankets strewn haphazardly across the expanse. The bed looked love-mussed. Instantly all of Julie's worst beliefs gathered together like stormclouds. What had really happened while she was gone?

She straightened the bed, then slowly toured the room. She told herself she was simply reacquainting herself with home, but she knew she was checking for small signs, anything to tell her whether "Cousin" Patsy had been here. Even when she found nothing, Julia wondered and worried. And despised herself for it.

Donning a pair of jeans and a beryl T-shirt with an imprint of a ring-necked pheasant and SOUTH DAKOTA on the left corner, Julie quickly dispensed several items from her case onto the dresser, then went into her former bedroom, where she unpacked the rest. She still nominally referred to this as her room and retained use of the closet. Turning to leave, her eye caught sight of a piece of paper held down by the phone on her nightstand.

It was a note written in a wide, loopy, schoolgirlish hand, thanking her for use of her room and telling her the sheets were freshly changed. It was signed *Patsy Stone.* Well, thought Julie as she tossed the note in the wicker wastebasket, surely that settled the matter. Surely her trust would bounce back now.

But it didn't.

A distant crackling sounded as Julie joined Cam in the kitchen. He glanced up, his lips tilting tenderly, his eyes darkly shining as they wandered over her slim figure. He stared as if he could devour her on the spot. Another rumbling discharge broke the spell.

"That storm's come back meaner than ever." He rolled his eyes. "Reminds me of the way you returned."

She laughed, but her gaze didn't meet his.

"I didn't make it to the store," he was saying now, his attention on whatever he was mixing together in a large yellow bowl. "So I hope you don't mind tuna salad."

Shaking her head, Julia crossed to the counter. She fought her need to look at him, but lost. With a sidelong glance she noted the way the untucked ends of his polo shirt flared each time he swept a spoon through the tuna mixture. The muscles in his arm bunched, then evened. She quickly looked away. A vision of that arm around Patsy flashed into her mind and a dull aching jealousy blunted her happier emotions.

She wasn't jealous of Patsy, not really. Basically she believed Cam's story. But Patsy was symbolic of the future. Of the time when Cam would leave her for the unknown someone. Today she'd attached Patsy's face and stunning figure to the unknown —and it tortured her. She had to stop tormenting herself, but how? Julia walked on wobbly legs to the china cupboard and began methodically setting the table. Her only protection in the past had been not to care. But she cared so much for Cam, it coursed with her blood.

Lightning electrified the world beyond their windows as they sat down to eat. Then the lights flickered, struggled, and surrendered to the storm, veiling Cam and Julie in darkness. She heard his warm laughter, the scraping of his chair. "Wait a minute. I'll get the candles," he said.

He ruffled her hair as he passed her chair. Julie's breath sucked in sharply, only to be released on a long, slow sigh when he was gone. She listened to his stumbling and grumbling from the netherworld beyond the darkened dining room. Wind howled into the silence. Rain beat furiously against the windows.

When he returned, he carried Grams's candelabrum in a pool of wavering light. The glow it cast softened his features, blurring the small lines etched beside his eyes and mouth and heightening the sensual cut of his lips, the length of his lashes. Julia stared, then forced her eyes to her salad. She was certain he could hear her heart thudding above the thunder and pelting rain.

The candlelight magically altered the atmosphere. They were bathed in memories of another candlelit night, memories that cast a warm spell over them. Julie found herself laughingly describing her trip, her parents, the old friends she'd seen. He reciprocated with a vivid recollection of the party he'd gone to while she was gone. And all the while they studied each other.

Cameron inspected the strands of silver the flames flicked into her hair. Odd, how such golden hair could look silver and amber and flaxen. He tipped his head to the side and leisurely took in each of her features: Her lustrous eyes with the drooping corners. Her small, straight, classical nose. Her wide mouth. He wondered how he'd ever thought her plain. She was lovely. And he loved her.

He wasn't certain just when he'd fallen in love with her. He rather suspected that it had been the night of the champagne bath when she'd been so utterly desirable and yet so untouchable. A night like this when he'd gazed at her in the muted radiance of flickering flames. Gradually the occurrence of the odd resentment he'd felt toward her in the beginning ceased. Then one night he'd found himself whispering "I love you" against the satin of her skin. Once he'd said it, he'd gone on saying it, not fully realizing how meaningful it had become. Now he knew it was the simple truth. He loved her.

A sliver of tuna slid from Julie's fork to rest on her lower lip. Before she could lick it away, Cam leaned forward and took it with a deft stroke of his tongue. He felt her quiver and leaned back, laughing softly.

"Julie, you delight me. Who would ever think that such a prim lady would dabble tuna on her lip?" He laughed, and his voice changed to a velvet caress. "The day I first saw you, I thought you'd be about as interesting as week-old news, but you constantly surprise me. I'm never sure what to expect with you."

He paused, and the flash of his gaze jarred her with a force to equal the lightning bolts outside. She knew she was blushing and wondered how he could still make her blush. He reached out and raised her chin. Her lashes fluttered against her cheek then lifted. She stared into the molten heat of his eyes and knew she loved him. That was all that mattered.

She ran her tongue around her lips. Her love was all that mattered. She could no longer deny it. To herself or to him. "Cam, I—" she whispered hesitantly.

"Do you know something, Julie?" he interrupted. He bore the air of one about to reveal a deep secret. "I've had more fun with you than I've ever had with anyone."

His voice rustled over her, then settled into her soul like a smothering shroud. *Fun.* She heard the word and stiffened. Was having fun the only thing men cared about? Didn't they care about responsibility, commitment, sharing sorrow as well? Her love wasn't what mattered. Cam's enjoyment was the yardstick of their relationship. The same measurement that had defined her relationship with Allen Kessler.

"I'm glad I've been so amusing," she said with a chill impassivity. She picked up her fork and resumed eating.

For once Julie's retreat to a cool reserve did not annoy Cam. He believed it stemmed from her fatigue, and possibly her earlier jealousy. Thinking of that, he grinned. Her display of jealousy had been nearly as good as a verbal admission of her love. He cheerfully swept her fork from her hand and laced their fingers together.

"You've been much more than that to me," he said as he stared into her uninviting gaze. "I don't have to tell you that."

She tried unsuccessfully to pull her hand from his. As his grip tightened, she ceased struggling. Her aloof resentment evaporated like cold mist in the steam of his steady gaze.

His eyes shifted to her hair, then down to her lips and lower still to her rapidly rising and falling breasts. At last his eyes returned to lock with hers. The naked desire in them made her tremble. "You're so . . . lovely. You can't imagine the wonder I feel whenever we make love, Julie. And the first time! I remember the first time. . . ."

Julie bent her head. Closing her eyes, she strained to call forth a vision of that first time. But she couldn't. That memory had been lost to her forever. Gradually, she realized he was still speaking.

"The way your blouse was misbuttoned. You looked so rumpled and ruffled, I wanted to rip your clothes off. And the way your skin glowed in the morning light—"

Her head shot up. "*Morning* light?"

He stopped, his mouth still parted. She could feel his breath reaching out to her. Candleflames outlined his lips as they slid up into a sheepish grin. "Well . . . yes."

Julia sat stock-still, staring at him in disbelief. He released her hand and sprawled back into the shadowed distance of his chair. The smile on his mouth appeared softer now. When she finally made her vocal cords function, her voice was hoarse. "But—but the party. . . ."

"You haven't got a head for alcohol, Julie," said Cam obliquely. Her eyes widened, then narrowed, then widened again. He began toying with his napkin.

"What are you saying? That night—didn't we . . .?"

"No," he interrupted shortly. With a placating smile, he explained, "Julie, you passed out. I put you to bed with me, but as I rather preferred to have you awake and responding, I didn't do anything more than hold you in my arms."

"But you let me think—let me think—" She sputtered into speechlessness.

"So what's the big deal?" he asked cheerfully. He leaned forward and Julia pulled back. "It's all worked out for the best. I love you. . . ."

"You tricked me!" she accused, leaping to her feet.

He stared up at her angry flushed face for a long time, then set aside the napkin. "It would have happened sooner or later, you know that."

She did, but she wasn't admitting it. "You knew I'd never go to bed with you, so you told me—"

"I told you the truth," cut in Cam. He rose slowly to his feet. "I told you we'd slept together. Which we had. You jumped to conclusions—"

"Only because you led me to those conclusions! I should have known! You're just as shallow as—"

"Julia!" He clamped his hands on her shoulders and gave her a light shake. "I admit I've wanted you—and intended to have you—from the start," he confessed calmly. "But I don't see why you're so upset. It's all worked out well, hasn't it? You can't deny you enjoy our lovemaking."

"You don't see why . . ." Again Julie's mouth worked soundlessly. She stared at his puzzled expression and longed to slap it from his face. Violence, however, was not in her nature. Instead, Julie wrenched from his clasp, spun, and raced blindly down the darkened hall. She slammed into her bedroom and buried her burning face in her hands.

She'd been duped! He wanted a bedmate and he'd made sure he got one! It made her sick to think how foolish, how naive, how trusting she'd been. She should have known Cameron would be like the rest: the predatory male animal out to get what he could. And he'd got it all right.

She heard the door open behind her. "Go away," she said, her voice muffled into her hands.

The door snapped shut. "I'm not going anywhere. Not before we've talked this out. If you want to leave, you'll have to go through me."

Peeking through her fingers, Julia squinted to see the dim reflection of his opaque outline in her dresser mirror. He was leaning against her door, his arms crossed over his chest and his legs planted slightly apart. Even in the inky light it was obvious he meant to stay. Damn him! She dropped her hands to form tight fists at her sides.

"You lied to me," she said stonily.

"It wasn't a lie precisely—"

"It wasn't the truth!"

"Okay. I'm sorry. But if I misled you, it was for your own good."

She whirled around at that. Her spine was rigid and her tone incredulous. "*My* good!"

"Sexual frustration isn't healthy. And don't try to tell me you weren't wanting me as much as I wanted you. I won't believe it. You couldn't respond to me the way you do—"

"Get out," said Julia, baring her teeth at him.

Seeing the gleam of her teeth, Cam's jaw set. He strove to control his rising temper. "I told you, I'm not going until we settle this."

"It is settled. I'm sleeping in my room, so kindly get out."

"If you're sleeping in here, then so am I. Accept that, Julie, because it's a fact."

She heard the finality in his voice and shivered. She knew that tone. It implied he expected to have his way. Just as he'd had his way from the start. He'd intended to have her from the first, he'd said. That meant all that talk about being "strictly roommates" had been calculated deception. Bitterness struck Julie with the same incessant fury of the rain pounding the earth outside. She wondered how many other deceits he'd practiced "for her own good."

"Here's another fact you can accept," he said after her long silence. "I love you. You're being unreasonable to ignore all the love we've shared the last few months because of a misunderstanding over when we first made love. Does it matter?"

"To me it does," she answered dully. She was thankful for the dark mantle that cloaked her mournful expression. "If you can't see that, then you don't understand me."

He came to her then and took her gently into his arms. "I *don't* understand you, Julia. Not in the least. But I love you, and I'm willing to try. I made a mistake, I admit that, and I'm sorry. Do you care enough to forgive me?"

She leaned against his chest, listening to the steady thump of his heart, feeling the warmth rise from his skin. In the mirror she saw the shadowy silhouette of their entangled embrace, and for a single moment she pretended this was the way they belonged together. She pretended the inevitable heartbreak would never come. But the moment passed, and Julie trembled with dread. All the heartache she'd envisioned again and again during the interminable afternoon at O'Hare would come true. It was only a matter of time.

Cam felt her shaking within his arms and wanted to kick himself for his stupidity in letting her know about the night of the party. Even so, he'd never dreamed Julie would react this way. He'd longed for what seemed a lifetime to hear her say she loved him. Her jealousy and ardor tonight had lifted him into an emotional security he now realized had been so much fantasizing. He'd been wrong. Julia didn't care the way he did. . . .

"Tell me what's wrong," he ordered softly. His breath stirred the blond wings of her hair.

"Allen," she whispered, then bit her lip as Cam inhaled sharply. She'd been thinking he would end by hurting her far more than Allen and had spoken without truly knowing it. She pushed away from Cam, only to be yanked back against his chest. She felt the sudden stillness of his stance.

"Who's Allen?"

"No one. Nothing. Forget I said anything," she pleaded quickly.

"Who's Allen?" he repeated. And again his voice held an undeniable command.

"A . . . guy I . . . dated . . . once. Before I met you."

Cam let this roll around his mind. A guy she'd dated. He knew there must be dozens of men she'd dated. But Allen was the one she thought of. That meant she'd loved this one. Had she seen him when she went back home? Was she still in love with him? Did all her uncharacteristic emotionalism tonight stem from this Allen? The thought was crushing. Cam had been hoping he was the cause of her volatile reactions. He was certain of one thing. He wasn't about to let some jerk from South Dakota waltz away with his woman. Julia was his, and Cam meant to keep her.

He didn't want to probe too deeply into this. He didn't want to hear her say she loved someone else. He would make her forget every man but himself. He would make her love him. His arms loosened gently. His hands moved in soft swirls up her spine. His lips caressed the silk of her hair. "Let's go to bed, dear one," he murmured and nudged her toward the door.

Julia didn't resist the pull of his arms. She couldn't even if she'd wanted to. She knew that as long as he wanted her, she would stay. She would stay until he finished breaking her heart.

In the morning, as much as he wanted to talk things out with Julie, Cam couldn't linger. Several important appointments awaited him at the office, and he fairly bolted from his shower to the front door, pausing slightly to graze Julie's brow with his lips. Instantly she wondered cynically why he felt such a need to be away from her. Hadn't she been *fun* enough?

Like weeds left untangled Julia's doubts and fears spread wildly, confusing her truer emotions. The only thing she could see clearly was her own inevitable pain. Each passing day added to Julie's dread of impending heartbreak. She knew it was stupid to anticipate the event, to taint her happiness with Cam with her dejection over their eventual breakup. But knowing how ridiculous she was didn't lessen her aching melancholy. Always thinking that this might be their last month, last week, last day, Julie eagerly awaited the moments they were together. At the same time it was soul-searingly painful to be near him. To be with Cam pierced her anew with the stabbing conviction that she was going to lose him.

When he spoke of love, Julie took it in like a dry sponge soaking up water, but still, she didn't believe him. He'd lied before. She didn't dare let herself hope he meant what he said. Hoping hurt too much.

She didn't think she could bear it. And yet she couldn't leave him. Not while he still wanted her. Her only protection would be a wall of pretense. She could pretend she wouldn't care when he left. No matter what it cost her to do it.

It cost the earth. To speak and smile, to act and react as if Cam weren't the axis of her universe. Never to show how her heart flipped when he walked into a room. To hide how her limbs trembled when he smiled. To bite back all the love, swallowing it like a bitter medicine, for her own good. It hurt over and over again. But Julie told herself it would hurt far more later, when she was alone.

Little by little she withdrew into a shell. Bit by bit, she learned to treat Cam as a stranger. A stranger with whom she still remained intimate. . . .

At first Cam tried teasing her from behind her shell, laughing and charming her into occasionally forgetting her guard. As she continued to maintain her impassive reserve he began losing his temper. "You're about as lively as a mausoleum at midnight," he snapped one night when she refused his offer of a movie.

Julia eyed him steadily without visible emotion. Inside she was wobbling like Jell-O rolling down a hill. She wasn't fun anymore. Soon he would tell her it was over. She spread her lips in a cool, thin smile. "You should have warned me being lively was a prerequisite of sharing this apartment with you. I would never have—"

But Cam had stalked out, banging the front door closed. She gnawed her lower lip. She hadn't meant to argue. Not that their icicle-brittle exchange could be called arguing. That would be much too warm a term for the gelid air that seemed to envelop them nowadays.

Julie began taking refuge in her work, staying later and later at the store. But even her beloved books didn't offer the solace she sought. She didn't know whether to feel hurt or relieved when Cam voiced no objections. It was, however, another proof that his interest was fading with the summer.

August hung over Chicago like an oppressive steambath. Day after day passed without the slightest breeze to stir the humid air. Heat stuck to her skin like melted bubble gum. Julia lifted the dampened ends of her hair away from her neck and stood before one of the two oscillating fans vainly battling the sticky heat in the bookstore.

"Go home, M.B.," she said for the third time. "If your face gets any more flushed, you'll be mistaken for a stoplight. I don't want you getting sick just because the air conditioning went out."

Mary Beth shrugged listlessly. Her frizzy black hair looked like a scrubbing pad, and her dark eyes had dulled to a stonelike opacity. Her freckles had been nearly erased by the heated flush over her skin. Being pregnant in the midst of a record-breaking heat wave left her feeling tired, spiritless. She couldn't find the energy to decide whether or not to go home.

Watching her knowingly, Julie looked around the empty store. Who was going to venture out in this heat to a shop with no air conditioning? "Get your purse, Mary Beth. I'm going to lock up the shop and drive you home. No protests," she said firmly. "I'll come back later and catch up on the bookwork."

"But you've been staying late every night," objected M.B. in a flat voice totally unlike her usual ringing tones.

Julie turned toward her office, hoping her flicker of guilt hadn't been seen. "Don't worry about it. Now, let's go."

Even the short distance across the parking lot to the car sent rivulets of sweat coursing down their backs. As she drove, Julie chattered constantly in an effort to cheer her friend. And to avoid the piercing memories of last night.

Last night. She wouldn't think about last night.

Smiling falsely at M.B., she demanded to know if they'd settled on names for the baby yet, then forced herself to listen. At the Farrows' apartment, Julia settled Mary Beth into a newly purchased secondhand wooden rocker and poured them each a tall glass of iced tea. She called the service company about the shop's conditioner and was again told no one could make it until after five at the soonest. "Which means overtime rates," she sighed to Mary Beth.

"Why don't you stay here for the afternoon, then go back just before he should arrive? At least you won't fry to death," said M.B., her spirits reviving in the cooled apartment.

"If you're sure it'd be okay."

"Of course. I'd like the company."

Julie pounded down a lump on the couch and sat. They talked for a time, drowsily discussing books and babies until the conversation drifted into silence. Leaning back, Julia closed her eyes and finally gave into the intrusion of last night.

The nights had become the hardest to endure. At night Julie struggled against surrendering to Cam's heated touch, his searing kisses. With each kiss he tore down a brick of her emotional barrier; each time it was that much harder to cement back into place. Their lovemaking lost all spontaneity. Her mind told her she was pushing Cam away, but she could no longer control the heavy depression stultifying her responses. It became a torment Julia both dreaded and craved.

It couldn't go on. This constant needing, yet fearing. Whenever she failed to restrain her response to him, she felt as guilty as if she'd slept with a man she didn't love. When she succeeded, she felt guilty for her failure to please Cam. She was a top spinning wildly out of control, dizzy and confused.

Knowing he would never come to bed before ten, Julia had gone to bed the instant she came home last night. She hoped fervently to be asleep before he joined her. She wasn't. She lay quietly, trying to breathe evenly. She felt the bed sag as his body pressed into place beside her.

"You don't have to pretend you're asleep," said Cam coldly. "If you don't want me, you only have to tell me."

She lay still a moment longer, her heart pounding violently, then she turned. "I—I wasn't pretending."

Julia was a poor liar. She saw Cam's disbelief in his gelid gaze. He stretched to turn out the bedside lamp and her mouth went dry at the flexing of his chest muscles. Darkness fell, and he slid down onto his pillow. She saw his silhouette outlined against the white linen and couldn't restrain her need to touch him, just once. She lay her fingertip against his cheek.

Cam flinched at her touch, and Julie jerked her finger back. "I'm sorry," she said in a thin whisper.

He said nothing, and the silence throbbed between them. Julie's muscles ached with the effort to remain immobile. She squeezed her eyes shut, but still she knew he was but a breath, a heartbeat, a fingertip away. She felt the heat of his body alongside hers. Each time he shifted even slightly, her disobedient heart lurched, then plunged when he did not reach for her.

Suddenly the broken spring creaked. Cam's body moved restlessly over hers. "Julia," he whispered on a moan.

His hands raced urgently over her flesh, kneading the pliant curve of her breast, pressing into the soft folds of her buttocks. Even in his fiercest passion, Cam had been gentle with Julie. This time, he was grabbing her, attempting to take what she seemed unwilling to give. While her desire rose up, wanting to meet his hunger, Julia's mind resented it. She resented his attempt to break through to her. She resented herself for wanting him to break through. She stoked up her hostility and lay silent, woodenly submitting to his insistent caresses.

As abruptly as he'd come to her, Cameron fell away. He rolled onto his pillow and stared up at the darkened ceiling. "Did you enjoy letting me wear myself out trying to heat you up?"

The acidity of his tone slashed her. "I'm sorry," she said in a voice barely audible. "I'm very . . . tired. I worked hard today and—"

"Forget it," he cut in. "Just forget it. Go to sleep."

"Cam, I—"

"Good night," he snapped, turning his back to her.

Tears stung the backs of her eyelids. Guilt, regret, sorrow, threatened to overwhelm her, but she battled not to let the tears fall. The shadows seemed to scream at her, calling her a fool. And she was, she knew it, but Julia didn't know what to do about it. She was caught in the web of her fears. That she'd spun it herself made no difference.

When she'd awakened, Cam was already gone. She dreaded seeing him tonight, facing the accusation in his eyes. But at least she had a legitimate excuse for delaying their inevitable meeting. She had to stay at the shop for the air-conditioning repair.

CHAPTER TWELVE

He knew before he answered who was calling. With a resigned sigh he picked up the phone. "Hello, Julie."

"Hello, Cam," she said.

"Working late again?" he asked, his voice hardening.

"Yes. You don't mind, do you?"

"Would it make any difference if I said yes? You'll stay there anyway. You practically live at that damn shop these days." He heard her quiet intake of breath. Everything she did nowadays was quiet, still, remote. "Why doesn't Mary Beth ever do any of the late work?" he inquired harshly.

"It's my job as manager. M.B. really isn't qualified. And besides, in her condition—"

"Pregnancy isn't a sickness." He waited, but she didn't react. He snapped the phone cord between his fingers. "Come home to me tonight, Julie."

"I can't," she began, but he hung up before she could explain.

He stood looking at the instrument, his fingers flexing with the desire to rip it out of the wall and hurl it into oblivion. After a moment he whirled out of the study and down the hall to the kitchen. He yanked a bottle of Scotch out of the cabinet and reached for a glass. Then he ignored it and swigged a generous gulp straight from the bottle.

What had gone wrong? It was a question Cam asked himself daily. When Julie had returned from South Dakota, she'd changed. She began gradually withdrawing. She returned to the reserved nunlike woman that he hated. He couldn't reach that woman. And the last two weeks she'd blatantly avoided him by working late at her damn bookstore.

Last night had been the worst. Remembering it, Cam downed another portion of Scotch. He thought of her lying unresponsive beneath his caress. He thought of how he'd lain, frustrated and aching from thigh to belly with the need to make Julia love him. But he had to face it. She not only didn't love him, she no longer wanted him physically.

What had gone wrong? That was his continual question. It all started with that damn vacation. Either her parents had influenced her or someone else had. *Someone else.* Cam froze in the act of putting the bottle up to his lips. There had been someone else. Someone named Allen.

But Allen was in South Dakota. Cam followed through with the bottle, swallowing another healthy mouthful of whiskey. Suddenly he choked on it. Gagging, he leaned over the sink and spit the expensive liquor over the stainless steel. When he straightened, his face was a pale mask.

My God, he thought, how gullible could I be? Working late every night! Working late, then coming home too tired to respond to his desire. The oldest line in the book, and he'd fallen for it—hook, line, and sinker. Not once had he suspected her of meeting someone else.

As he braced against the counter, he imagined Julie's long silky legs entwined with some other man's. Rage blurred his vision. He wasn't going to stand by and let Allen run off to South Dakota with her. He tore from the kitchen and out to his car. He drove like a maniac still confined to a straitjacket. Something in him still hoped he was wrong, and it was that hope he focused upon as he wove in and out of rush-hour traffic.

Tires screeched in protest as he jammed to a halt in the small graveled space behind the row of buildings housing the Bookshelf. Cam's heart plummeted and his rage leaped at the realization that Julie's dented blue Toyota wasn't in the lot. He banged on the back door, then went around to peer through the barred glass in the front. No one was there. The shop was closed.

He employed several minutes cursing a blue cloud and comforting himself with the thought of wringing her neck. His white-hot fury gradually spent itself, and as he cooled Cam began to think that perhaps Julie had gone home. He hadn't given her a chance to speak—maybe she'd responded to his summons to come to him. He may have passed her on the way to the shop. The way he'd been driving, he wouldn't have noticed an eighteen-wheeler unless he'd run into it. Feeling more confident, he returned to his car and made his way back to the apartment on the Drive.

When he arrived there, however, his worst suspicions were confirmed. Julia wasn't home. She wasn't at the shop. She had to be with her lover.

He should have seen it coming. She'd been so cool to him, so detached and uncaring. He grabbed the Scotch and sank into one of the wingback chairs. He took a long pull at the bottle and devised one method of confronting her with her infidelity. When he realized his vision was ending with his smothering her in forgiving kisses, he refortified himself with another swig. But the idea of throwing her out didn't make him feel any better. His fingers beat restlessly against the glass bottle and he wished he knew where to go after her. Where was she?

Where was he? Julia asked herself impatiently. She looked at the slim band on her wrist. It was now past seven, and the repairman still hadn't shown up. She wanted to go home! The yearning in Cam's voice as he'd said, "Come home to me," had wrenched at her. When he'd hung up on her, she'd called the service company to reschedule. But the company had informed her that it was tonight or next week.

"I'm sorry, ma'am, but with this heat, conditioners are conkin' out all over town. And I gotta take appointments as they call in. If my boy don't come out tonight, you're gonna have to wait."

She'd agreed with a heavy sigh, then hung up. "He says tonight or nothing," she explained as she turned to M.B. "We can't let the books go without temperature control that long, so I'd better get back to the shop."

Mary Beth tactfully refrained from asking why Julie wanted to change the repair appointment in the first place. Instead, she volunteered to call Cam and explain Julie's delay.

"No!" exclaimed Julia. "I mean, really, there's nothing to explain, Mary Beth. I don't have to explain my actions to him, anyway. He's just my roommate, remember."

"If you say so," said M.B., sounding thoroughly unconvinced. "At least let me send some supper with you." She pushed herself out of the rocker, grinned, and said merrily, "I think it's twins. They don't kick in rhythm."

They laughed and put together a light salad and cucumber sandwiches, then packed some ice and two pop-top cans of soda in a cherry-red cooler. As soon as she returned to the shop Julie had eaten the sandwich and picked at the salad. She was now drinking the second can of soda. Several times her eyes strayed toward the phone. But she couldn't quite work up the resolve to call Cam. She avoided confrontations, hoping to avoid the moment he would declare it was time for her to move out.

A rattling at the door broke in on her latest debate over whether to call or not to call. She let the repairman in amid a vapor of gray cigar smoke. He started talking at the crack of the door and continued all through the shop.

"I've been in the business twenty-two years and never been out on so many emergency calls as this week. Twenty-two years! This heat's somethin' else! My name's Samson T. Beard, and I can tell you I've never seen heat like this."

He shook his head, which Julia thought was gray but couldn't tell through the swirling smoke. She longed to tell him to put the offensive cigar out, but she feared he would leave without doing his job. Trying not to inhale, she pointed out the conditioner. He immediately launched upon a history of his family, his wife's family, his brother's family, all without seeming to notice or care if Julia paid the least attention. When she finally managed to slip back to her office, she still heard him clucking and whistling and telling her what a mess her aluminum coils were in. "Should've had copper!" she heard him yell just as the phone rang.

"Hello, Bookshelf," she said. A long silence punctuated with her own breathing echoed in her ears. "Hello?" she tried again.

"So you're there," said Cam, his tone distinctly accusing.

"Of course, I'm here," she returned. "I told you I would be."

"Yes. That's what you told me."

His anger pulsed through the receiver to slap at Julia. She stared at the phone as if it might tell her what the problem was. Then she cleared her throat. "Uh, is there something you wanted, Cam?" She was distracted by a call from Samson and put her hand over the mouthpiece to reply, "Just a minute, please!" Turning back, breathlessly anxious to placate him, she begged, "Can you hold on a minute? I'll be right back."

He heard the phone drop, then a distant rumbling and a string of oaths. To Cam it was unintelligible, but he knew it wasn't Julie's voice coming through the wire. Those deep tones were all male. He clenched the empty bottle in one hand and the phone in the other. Abruptly he slammed both forcefully down, smashing the bottle and jangling the phone. It was precisely what he meant to do to Allen when he got to the bookshop.

Julie returned to the phone to discover the line had been cut off. Cam had hung up on her again! She shook with a flaring violent rage. She knew her anger was irrational, out of proportion to the incident, but her pent-up emotions needed release. With a whirl she dashed a stack of notecards to the floor, then kicked aimlessly at them before bending to pick them up. If only Cam were here, she'd teach him not to keep hanging up on her!

Samson T. Beard appeared in a puff of cigar smoke. "I've done what I can, ma'am."

"The air conditioner is working?"

"Yeah. Can't guarantee there won't be another overload with this heat, but should do right enough now. Just keep it at an even temperature, not too low. Now my brother Willie's third wife . . ." he started on another round of family history while Julia politely urged him toward the exit.

At last she locked the door behind him, wondering briefly if the *T* stood for *Talkative.* She switched off all but one light at the back, then clicked her teeth at the haze that streaked the moonlight filtering through the windows. Cigar smoke clumped between the bookshelves, obscuring the musty odor she loved so well. She sprayed air freshener throughout the stacks, with little success in dispelling the vapor. She could only hope the ventilation system would soon send the smoke into oblivion. The heavy stench even clung to her clothes. As she was turning out the lights she remembered a work shirt she kept for doing chores in the dusty basement. She could at least change out of her smelly blouse before going home to face her contentious roommate.

Within minutes she'd found it lying on a roller-cart in the bowels of the basement. She shook it out and threw it on, rolling the sleeves up to her elbows as she mounted the stairs. She was fastening the first button in place when she heard the pounding at the front door.

Her first thought was of Samson T. Beard and his smelly cigar. With a moue of dismay she clasped the wrinkled edges of her shirt together and advanced toward the impatient battering. "Hold on! I'm coming!" she called, then halted, struck motionless at the sight of an extremely hostile Cameron Stone glowering at her from the other side of the pane.

Cam's raised fist hung in midair as he took in the sight of Julie, *his* Julie, hastily donning an oversized man's blue work shirt. Fury roared in his ears. He brutally pummeled the door.

"Julia! Let me in! Now!"

She took an obedient step forward, then stopped. Let him in? How dare he bellow at her like that! He had no cause to be angry with her. *He* was the one who'd hung up on *her*! Forgetting the undone buttons of her shirt, Julia let her hands fall to her sides, clenched into tight balls. An expanse of flesh glimmered in the faint illumination. Cam growled and Julie gasped. Clutching the faded blue front together, she spun around and stalked purposefully to the back of the shop.

"Dammit, Julia! Let me in or I'll break this damn door!" threatened Cam on a violent blare.

She ignored him. She calmly picked up her purse from the counter, then the brass ring of keys that lay beside it. A clattering thunder resounded as Cam threw his shoulder against the door. Her facade of composure evaporated as she watched him brace his body for a second ramming. He couldn't possibly intend to break in!

He could.

Whether she was prompted by concern for the door or Cam's shoulder, Julie didn't know. But as he lunged a well-executed body block toward the entrance, she reached for the release below the counter. At the moment his side crashed against the door, her finger pressed that button.

The door flew open beneath the impact of his weight and Cam sprawled with a grunt onto the floor. Julie was still angry and not a little frightened, but the sight of him flailing to the floor with a look of shock stamped over his features proved to be too much for her. Clamping a hand over her mouth, she began laughing. He shook his head dazedly and sprang up. She laughed harder. He frowned furiously and started toward her. She doubled over, gasping for breath.

"Oh, God, you looked so, so—" was all she managed before going off into another machine-gun crack of laughter.

It was the liveliest she'd been for weeks, and Cam couldn't resist the beauty of her sparkling laughter. The idea of breaking her neck dissolved with her merriment. With a strong effort he tamped down his rising desire and remembered why he'd come. He advanced and demanded hotly, "Where is he?"

Her laughter withered like a flower denied water. "Who?"

"Don't play games!" he barked. Cam pivoted away from her and began prowling through the stacks. His hands opened, then closed, betraying his urgent wish to throttle someone. "You can't deny you had a man here—or do you expect me to believe you've taken up smoking cigars?"

Julie stared at him in honest bewilderment. "Of course, I don't expect—"

He wheeled sharply. "And button that damn shirt!" Then he was barreling down the basement steps before she could express any of the stinging retorts that were dangling on her tongue. Just who did he think he was, bursting in here and ordering her about like that? She buttoned the shirt in short, angry jerks, then stood at the top of the steps awaiting him.

"You forgot to turn out the lights," she said coldly as he came up.

He mouthed an obscenity that took her breath away. "What did he do? Sneak away?"

As she looked into his eyes Julia's tongue weighted uselessly in her mouth. Woven into his anger was a visible wounded pain, a pain she knew she'd caused.

He grabbed her shoulders and shook her roughly. "If he cared for you, he'd have stayed. Can't you see that? And he wouldn't make you suffer a cheap hole-in-the-corner affair. He's not worth your love, Julie."

Her head was flopping from side to side, tossing her thoughts into a jumbled heap. It was only when Cam abruptly released her that she understood what he had been saying. She didn't think through to the cause behind his incredible accusations. She simply realized what he'd said and reacted in one surge of fury.

"How dare you say such things to me," she raged. "Even your obvious state of inebriation doesn't excuse such insults."

"I am not," he bit out through clenched teeth, "inebriated."

"Ha! I could pass out just from inhaling your breath," Julie shot back. "And for the record, Mr. Stone, the only cheap affair I've suffered is with *you*!"

"There's no need for you to continue this deception, Julia," he returned in a strained staccato. "I know all about Allen. But I don't understand how you could sneak around behind my back. If you wanted to leave me for him, you should have done so openly, not like this." He indicated the shop, her shirt, her sticky dishevelment in one disparaging gesture.

Her mouth dropped open, but nothing came out. To Cam her astonishment appeared to be shock. Shock that he'd discovered the truth. A despairing anger coursed through him. He hadn't felt such an impotent fury since he was six—left helplessly, hopelessly angry at a mother who was no longer there. How could Julia do this to him? He wanted to inflict an equal hurt upon her and knew he had to leave before he did so.

He pushed past her and disappeared between tall tiers of shelves crammed with old books. Julia pressed her fingertips into her temples. What on earth was he talking about? Why would he think Allen had been here? How could he possibly think she'd even look at another man? His charges were ridiculous! She should be indignant, offended. She *should.*

She moved slowly to follow him, torn between the vestiges of her anger and a trembling uncertainty. He'd sunk onto the padded cushion of a short bench. She stood just beyond his reach. "What are you raving about?" she asked quietly.

"Allen."

The brusque reply had the odd effect of erasing the last of her animosity. Julie sat down on the bench, being careful not to touch Cam. "I don't know what this is all about." She caught the skeptical look he cast at her and went on levelly, "I haven't seen Allen in over two years. And if I wanted to leave you, it certainly wouldn't be for him."

His head swiveled. Even in the dim shadows, she could see the questioning hope flaring in his eyes. "If . . .?"

"I don't want to leave you." Julia took a deep breath and plunged in. "I thought *you* wanted to leave me."

He looked stunned. "You what?"

"I thought—I thought you weren't interested anymore. That you were getting ready to tell me it was over," she whispered, bowing her head.

He continued to stare at her with the look of a man confronting a sideshow freak. "How could you think I'd do anything so stupid?"

Swaths of blond hair flared as she shook her head. He caught a silken strand and laced his fingers through it. She kept her gaze averted. Within the ample folds of the faded work shirt, her bosom rose and fell rapidly. His own heart raced to match that tempo.

"Julia," he murmured gently, "I love you."

She sat very still. This time she believed him. The pain she'd seen in his eyes proved without a doubt that he loved her. But no surge of joy warmed her chilled heart. He may love her, but not enough, not enough.

Letting her hair slip through his fingers, Cam said slowly, "Right from the start I knew I wanted you." He saw Julie's almost imperceptible flinch and went on quickly. "But I resented you too. Always at the times I most wanted you, I most resented you. For a long time I didn't understand it, but . . . I think I resented you because I knew right from the first that I was going to love you. I didn't want to, I fought like hell not to, but I do. Do you believe that, Julie?"

"Yes," she said at last. Her voice quavered. "But for how long? How long do I have until you want to love someone else? Someone more *fun*?"

He cradled her head between his palms and forced her to meet his gaze. "What do you mean? There's no one else!"

Her agonized look clearly said *Not yet.*

"Are you saying you want marriage, is that it?"

She didn't speak, but he saw the answer in her eyes. His fingers tightened against her cheekbones. "Julie, Julie, you can't seriously believe marriage guarantees love will last."

She reached up and pulled his hands down. Her fingers played nervously over the dusting of hair along the back of each. "No. I don't think that. I know love has no guarantees. But I do believe that marriage proves a willingness to try, a willingness to make a relationship last through bad times as well as good. Whether marriage works or not, it's a commitment to *try.*"

His silence oppressed her. She'd bared her heart, her soul, and he obviously didn't love her enough to make the commitment her love needed to survive. She dropped his hands and started to rise. He grasped her elbow and yanked her back down.

"Who was smoking cigars here? Who did I hear cursing on the phone?"

His abrupt change of subject annoyed her. She wanted to scream at him, but the core of her spirit had wilted. Like a litany, her mind repeated again and again, He doesn't love me enough. She felt numb, but she forced her lips to part, the words to come. "A repairman. The air conditioning went out. Which I would have told you if you hadn't kept hanging up on me," she explained, a brittle barb in the last statement.

"What have you been doing each night the last two weeks?"

"Working. You know that." Julia stared at the books lining the shelf in front of her. They were sitting in the history section, and she focused on *The Letters of Henry Adams* as if it were of consuming interest. She felt Cam's eyes rake over her.

"Do I?" he queried tensely. "I was beginning to think you were punishing me."

Her head whipped round. "Punishing you! But why—"

"That's what I couldn't figure out. You've been treating me like a stranger—"

"Some stranger!" she broke in with a shaky laugh.

He ran his fingertip along her jaw and down the curve of her throat. He felt her shiver and bent to place his lips where his finger had been. "But you've been so cool, so distant toward me, I could only think you didn't care any longer."

"Oh, Cam. . . ." Julie shuddered as he kissed the tip of her earlobe. "I—I didn't *want* to care! I thought if I could convince myself I didn't care, it wouldn't hurt so much when you left me. Only it's hurt so much *more*!"

"For a smart lady you've been incredibly dumb," stated Cam with a warm satisfaction that turned the insult into an endearment. He circled her neck with his hand, letting his thumb monitor her quickening pulse.

She lay her palms against the width of his thigh and said softly, "I—I love you."

With a low groan he pulled her onto his lap and kissed her fiercely. His fingers dug into the swell of her hip. He could feel her erratic heartbeat against his chest. His desire rose up and he scooped her to him as he stood. "I need you," he moaned softly. He lay with her on the sloping wood floor.

"Now?" she laughed unsteadily.

"Now."

The aromas of aging paper and seasoned leather mingled with the whiskey on his breath as he wildly sprinkled random kisses over her face. His fingers skimmed through her hair, and Julie felt her tingling need matched in his trembling touch. She traced the structure of his jaw with her darting fingers, then softly stroked the outline of his mouth. His tongue teased the tips of her fingers, twirling her nerve endings beyond control. Unrestrained excitement vaulted through her, and she whispered on a breathless laugh, "You've got to be drunk or mad or both."

Shifting his weight to the side, one leg thrown over hers, the other resting tautly against her thigh, Cam began undoing her shirt. He paused at the third button and bent to kiss the curve of her breast. She quivered in response. He lifted his head to gaze at her from beneath half-closed lids. Her hair splayed out in a golden fan, her lashes shadowed her cheek, her lips parted in passionate anticipation. As he watched, her eyelids slowly rose. He saw desire, love, and puzzlement in her eyes.

"Julie, I'm willing," he said in a ragged voice.

"Willing?" she echoed hoarsely. He was burning her with his searing gaze. Her body cried out to be touched and kissed in all the ways he knew to perfection. She could feel the throbbing hardness of his own desire against her thighs. So why was he waiting, staring at her that way?

"To try to make our love last a lifetime. I'm willing to marry you."

Her reaction startled them both. She bolted upright, shoving him off-balance, and cried, "No!"

They stared at each other, stunned dismay reflected on both faces. "What the hell do you mean?" demanded Cam finally as he righted himself.

Julie wrung her hands, looking away from him. "I can't let you marry me."

"Can't? What do you mean, can't?" His voice rose with each word, ending on a shout that rang in her ears.

"It wouldn't be right," she said uncomprehendingly. She tried to scramble to her feet, but Cameron effectively foiled her attempt by flinging himself on top of her. Her breath was knocked from her with an "Oooff," and he took immediate advantage of her speechlessness.

"Listen to me, Julia Hollis," he said in his most commanding tones. "Whatever stupid notions have come into your head, get rid of them. If you've met someone else, forget him. I'm the only man for you and we're getting married."

"We can't!" she wailed.

"Why not?"

His lips were white at the edges. Julia wanted desperately to kiss his rage away, but she knew she couldn't let him make this sacrifice. She blinked her tears back and willed herself to speak. "Willing isn't the same as wanting. You don't *want* to marry me, not really. You'll be marrying to please me, not yourself! It wouldn't be right! You'd resent me for it in the end. I can't let you sacrifice your freedom—"

"Shut up, Julie," he cut in.

She disregarded this curt directive. "I'll always feel guilty for having forced you into—"

Cam clapped his hand firmly over her mouth, stifling her further objections. "I'm not being forced into anything." His tones softened and he lifted his hand to gently touch her cheeks. "Marrying you will please me very much, Julia."

"It will?" Her voice clearly conveyed her doubt of this.

"It will," he affirmed. "I couldn't bear to go through another month like this last one. Or a night like tonight! Do you have any idea what torment I went through thinking you were meeting another man? The images I conjured up were worse than nightmares." He laughed mirthlessly into the curve of her neck. "Julie, dear one . . . I can't bear the thought of anyone else ever touching you. I want you to be mine. Forever. As my wife."

"Are you . . . sure?"

"Let me show you how sure I am," he murmured in reply. He pressed her against the floor and brought his mouth to hers in a kiss so piercingly passionate, the embers of Julie's doubts were finally, totally extinguished. There could be no doubt of his desire—or of his love.

Shadows meandered through the shelves to blanket them. Their loving this night was fragile, a delicate exploration of love fully given and received. As two bodies came tenderly together, two souls melded into one.

They lay in hushed wonderment. Julie's heart clamored against Cam's until she thought it would burst with the joyous drumming. When he finally pulled away, he saw the glistening track of tears sliding down her cheek. He traced the path with his fingertip.

"Why are you crying?" he queried in quick concern. "Do you dislike the idea of marrying me that much?"

"No!" she denied vehemently, clasping her arms around his

back. She turned her head and gently caught the tip of his finger between her teeth. She tasted her happy tears on his skin, then said with quiet joy, "I want to marry you more than anything."

"Then why are you crying?"

Julia kissed his fingertips as they lingered over her lips. "I was just thinking how happy you've made one person."

"You?" he whispered huskily.

"No," she said, her lips beginning to curve in the beautiful smile that always dazzled him. "My mother."